ABOUT THE AUTHOR

Brian Jarman was born on a farm in Mid-Wales, the joint youngest of five brothers. After studying in London, Paris and Cardiff, he joined the South Wales Argus as a reporter and then worked for the BBC for 22 years, mainly as a current affairs editor for World Service. He's now Senior Lecturer in Journalism at London Metropolitan University. He's published three other novels: **The Missing Room, The Fall From Howling Hill,** and **The Final Trick.**

Published by Fitzrovia Books, London

Copyright © 2018 by Brian Jarman

Front cover drawing © 2018 by Andrew Radkowsky

All rights reserved

ISBN-13: 978-1726116718
ISBN-10: 1726116719

REVIEWS FOR THE MISSING ROOM

I loved it. Its a fine novel, very well plotted, full of character, and I couldn't put it down.
Carmen Callil, founder of Virago Press

An ingenious page turner, but with the power to encourage reflection on the human condition - it's all there: family, health, career, and of course the slippery slope to alcoholism.
Clive Jennings, Director of the National Print Gallery

Simply on the strength of a piece of fiction about ME from a male point of view, Jarman deserves 5 stars. And, there is a lot more. The writing is strong - Mr. Jarman is not only a fine journalist but a great storyteller.
Pamela Post-Ferrante, writer and lecturer

AUTHOR'S ACKNOWLEDGEMENTS

Special thanks to my trusty editor, Annabel Hughes, and to Andrew Radkowsky for the cover drawing and for his most helpful suggestions

This book is dedicated to the wonderful memory of
Aldouina Radkowsky-Guerrini, who grew up in Gradoli,
and to the Radkowsky and Guerrini families

The Absent Friend

By Brian Jarman

Gradoli, Early May

As the sun begins to slip behind the distant hills, I position myself on the small balcony, camouflaged by *caprifoglio* (honeysuckle), and sip my *aperitivo*. I watch the swallows swoop and swirl around the *piazza* in their mad farandole heralding the night. I marvel daily at their synchronicity, their ability to avoid splodging the walls of the *palazzo*. I say *palazzo* because that's what the building is now called – the *Palazzo Mancini*. But the locals still call it *La Rocca* – the fort. Not that you'd recognise it as a medieval fortress – it's been added to and altered so much over the years. Now it's a hodge-podge of flats of all shapes and sizes.

I'd never paid much attention to swallows before we came here, not even when I was a child on the farm in Mid Wales. But now it's the time I like best, until that yappy little mop of a dog lollops on to the balcony next door. Then I go inside.

God knows what they must make of me down below, the women (crones, K used to call them) on their chairs and stools one side of the square, the men on the bench opposite:a wan Welshman wearing sunglasses, sitting alone behind the leaves, with only the occasional glint of light on his glass to show that he's still awake.

Not that they know I'm Welsh, or British for that matter. The flat used to belong to a French couple, known to all and sundry around here as *i francesi*. When K and I first came here the crones saw no reason to change the habit and we became *i francesi* too. In the early days we tried to enlighten them. One morning before going out for the day, we went to put our rubbish bags in the huge green wheeled bins in the far corner of the piazza by the archway that leads out into the town. We had yet to learn the etiquette of the bins. We had with us a five-litre glass flagon which we were going to fill up in the local winery. You just drive up and pour the local wine into your receptacle from a nozzle, like filling up a tank of petrol. You hand over a few euros and off you go. A couple of crones sitting on the bench nearby spotted the flagon. We never did by the way find out why so many of them live alone in the flats in the *palazzo,* apart from the fact they were so cheap. These particular ones we knew as the Guardians of the Garbage as they sat there policing the bins and ticking you off if you put in anything you shouldn't. They must have thought we were going to put the flagon in the rubbish bin, whereas glass had to be recycled. I could hear them muttering '*i francesi*' and '*bottiglia.*' I smiled at them and said, '*Non siamo francesi, siamo inglesi.*' I didn't even bother with '*galesi*' as I thought Welsh would probably sound extraterrestrial to them. The crones nodded and smiled - or maybe grimaced is the more appropriate word. But we were forever *i francesi.*

A few weeks after that we'd returned from a day out to Florence or Siena one evening. The car, especially the roof, was speckled with bugs. I suddenly had one of my brainwaves and decided the easiest way of cleaning it was with a mop. So I set to with a bucket of soapy water outside the front door. This proved to be as good as a circus for the crones and co and served to confirm to them, if confirmation were needed, our insanity. One of them came and grabbed the mop and made mopping motions along the ground as if to show me what it was for.

The only young woman of the *palazzo,* and owner of the yappy dog, was sitting with her young daughter – five or six I would say. The girl was transfixed. The mother must have signalled it was time for bed and her daughter kicked up a fuss, wanting to stay and watch. I caught the words *francesci, lavare* and *macchina.* She wanted to watch the French people wash their car. What she got was a hard smack on the back of her legs and she was dragged off howling. So right from the start we didn't fit in. We never mastered the shutter etiquette, for example. All the shutters round here are green (In Rome they're grey; somewhere else they'd be brown). They match the panes in your windows so if there are two small ones at the top, there'll be corresponding shutters. And within the shutters there are panels which you prop open without having to open the whole shutter. It's all very complicated. And the locals have a way of opening them in certain ways at certain times of the day as the sun follows its course. They're all in sync. Except for ours, of course. They're all over the place. Another sign of our ineptitude, no doubt.

A week or so after the mop incident, K had run out of space in our tiny kitchen and put a saucepan on the window to dry. I went in and knocked the window as I passed, so the saucepan fell off onto the terrace below. We rushed down to find the flat belonging to the terrace – no easy task because of the jumble of flats and add-ons. In the end we had to go out of our front door, down a little side alley, up a few steps and in another front door before we found it. A very angry crone had already recovered the battered pan. We couldn't really see what the fuss was about, and were just relieved it hadn't hit anybody. But we explained and apologised profusely. She was unmoved.

'In *our* country we do not throw saucepans through the window,' she said, or words to that effect. As if she thought it were common practice in England. Or France, rather. Still, it would provide a news item for discussion in the *piazza* that evening.

We thought they were so picturesque and romantic when we first came, the crones and the old men, sitting outside and taking in the last of the sun. There was something so peaceful, solid, eternal about them. They were from another age. It was only when we got used to them and picked up a bit more of the lingo that we realised they were in fact gossiping about anyone who passed as soon as they were out of sight: the way she hung out her washing, the place he parked his car. But we'd grown to love it by then, K and I, so we didn't mind.

We'd picked up the habit of going for an evening stroll, a *passeggiata,* arm in arm like the locals. We'd stop for our *aperitivo* outside the small cafe up the narrow passage opposite the arch. The manageress who rejoices in the name of Regilda would bring us out olives or nuts or some such to go with our drinks, and chat a while. Glad of the company no doubt, after an afternoon of virtually no custom.

Then we'd settle down and watch others take their *passeggiata* in turn. Elderly mainly. The young had followed their brothers and sisters to Rome or Milan in search of work. Gradoli is off the beaten track, as you would say, on a little side road that leads down to the lake and what we came to know as Condom Cove. We'd driven down there one afternoon in the early days, parked the car by the ice cream hut and spread the travel rug on the grass by the shore, only to spot two or three used condoms in the near vicinity. We were too lazy and content to move after our *porchetta* – delicious cold pork stuffed with fennel seed - and Chianti. We lay in the sun, listening to the water lap and the ducks quack.

We used to drive a lot then: to Siena, Florence, Orvieto and Rome, of course, but also in the hills around the lake, discovering little towns like Civita di Bangoreggio, now dubbed *Civita che Muore* (The Dying City). Built entirely on one of those old volcanic outcrops and reached only by one perilous looking bridge to the hill opposite, the village is now slowly crumbling away. Almost all the inhabitants have left. A smattering of the older ones have stayed to scrape up whatever pickings they can from the odd tourist who dares to cross the bridge.

I remember one old woman sitting on a little stool in front of her garden gate, quietly inviting us to visit her garden round the back with a sad smile and a swish of her hand. A lovely garden it was too, unusually green for this part of the country, with stunning views of the surrounding hills and valleys from its precarious hilltop perch. When we left she smiled sadly again and held up her apron for any coins we might like to toss her way.

On the way home from these outings K would make her quaint observations of the passing landscape in her vivid and imaginative way. The pines were umbrella trees, the cypresses were open umbrella trees. Everything was new to us then, worthy of comment. The first time we drove to Siena K said, 'Oh look! How sweet, the little schoolchildren are waving at us.' She waved back.

It was only then that I caught sight in the mirror of a 1920s Bugati racing car, its driver in a leather helmet and goggles looking rather menacing. We were in the middle, or rather at the front, of the Rome-Siena Vintage Car Rally. It didn't stop K from insisting on having a pee on the roadside though. When K had to go, she had to go.

'Find a little lane or lay-by or something where I can go behind the bushes,' she commanded.

I drove on, not finding one.

'Stop! Stop now.'

'But there's no...'

'STOP!'

I pulled in at a gateway – stone pillars and iron gate. Must have led to a farm or a manor house or something. She got out and squatted down. She tried to hide behind the car but a couple of the vintage drivers spotted her and honked. She gave another merry wave. It gave the day a surreal, slapstick, Keystone Cops kind of feel.

As time went on, we didn't venture so far afield. K was less and less up to it. We'd still manage to stroll up to the Caffe degli Amici for our *aperitivo*. Just over the terrace you could glimpse a corner of the lake, around from Condom Cove. You couldn't see much of it, unlike our living room which has sweeping views over the lake. Our one true friend, the historian and Communist Party activist, Giulio, once told me it was the deepest lake in Europe. I couldn't quite believe it. Isn't it that one in Russia - Lake Baikal? I once went past it on the Transiberian Express. It was early in the morning and foggy so you couldn't see much. No, that would be in Asia. Still, I'm not sure that Lago di Bolsena is the deepest. Maybe he meant the deepest volcanic one. Still, he was a fount of knowledge about the region and its history and customs.

From the Caffe deli Amici you couldn't see the two islands – the Tintin Islands, K called them. And indeed they do look like something Hergé might have drawn, their sheer rocky cliffs plunging down from their woody tops into the blue water.

It's still my favourite time of day, when the swallows dance. We always had a sense of serenity on that terrace by the cafe, even when tragedy struck. May's my favourite month here too. Bugger England in April. I do think of Mays on the farm back in Wales though. They all seem glorious, when for the first time summer seemed a real possibility after the bitter winter. They all merge into one: long, still, hazy days, their silence broken only by birdsong, the hum of insects in the woods, the bleat of a gambolling lamb. From our top field above the farmhouse, everything you could see would be graded shades of blue or green; the sky, the distant hills, the valley meadows, the bluebell sheen carpeting the woods.

For yes, I'm afraid I am now given to the occasional reminiscence, although I try not to be too sentimental about it. Each generation must think that summers were idyllic when they were young. My father used to say you could hang up your coat in May and not take it down till September, when he was a boy. You could time it almost to the day by the swallows, he'd say. They'd arrive on his mother's birthday, April 19th or a couple of days afterwards and stay until his father's on September 24th or thereabouts. They'd been nesting in the same place since he was a boy – in the loft above the stables. The talent, he would have called it. One year they forgot to open the door to the talent and the swallows stayed on the wires outside and chirped until they were let in.

The talent! I've just remembered that word, after all these years. Isn't it odd how long-buried memories suddenly unearth themselves? I've no idea whether the word was from English or Welsh, whether it was just our name for that loft or a real word, or even how to spell it. (Talant?) But just thinking of it summoned up a lost world: a different universe, gone forever but still here, a parallel time.

Now where am I? Swallows, that's it. But not in the talent. I couldn't give two hoots about them then. Here in the *piazza*, when K was here. Maybe they come from the same place in Africa as the swallows in Wales. It's amazing to think that they can fly for thousands of miles and end up every year in the exact same spot.

After we finished our *aperitivo* at the Caffe degli Amici, K and I would saunter back to the flat and make dinner, maybe stopping off at Mrs Mould's to get some odd or end we needed. K had christened her Mrs Mould because she had a trick of waylaying you as you went past, beckoning in a conspiratorial way, whispering that she had some beautiful fresh peaches, or asparagus, or mushrooms. It was as if she were doing you a huge favour and you weren't to tell anyone else. It was only when you got home that you discovered the fresh peaches or whatnot on top of the brown paper bag hid a rotting mush underneath. She always seemed to manage to sell you four times the amount you needed to boot.

We never had the heart to complain. She couldn't have made much, poor old soul. We just tried to avoid buying too much there, especially anything *fresco*. But her cartons of wine were handy when you'd run out. And K liked a certain kind of waffley cake she sold.

Then we'd sometimes chat to Giulio as he exercised his dog Silvia on the grass at the *palazzo*. She was an old gal, but would bound up as fast as she could to see us. K loved her. We were crestfallen when Giulio announced nonchalantly that she'd died.

I never go inside Mrs Mould's now, or to the Caffe degli Amici very much. The Cafe of Friends. Maybe because I don't really have any. A few acquaintances perhaps. But they're enough. I don't even keep in touch with people in London or Wales. From our daughter Alex in Australia we get the Christmas Card (even the Australian ones have snow and sleighs and robins), the photos of the kids recording another year's growth, and those dreadful round-robin letters which bore the crap out of me, Grandad, so God knows what it does to everybody else on their computerised list.

Our son Jake we hardly ever saw even when we all lived in London. He's been over here a couple of times on largely unsuccessful trips. We didn't even know how to make small talk, as strangers do. As for old friends, many had moved out of London over the years, seeking serener lives or better schools in the Home Counties or by the sea.

Those left in London had sort of run their course, with a couple of notable exceptions. I'd fallen out with my best friend David and never saw him. The less said about that the better. Most of the ones that were left were more K's friends than mine, and I'd began to tire of the endless round of dinner parties with the same faces and same mouths spouting the prescribed liberal opinions, however forcibly and indignantly they were expressed. And that dreadful competition of who'd seen the latest exhibitions, plays, films, read the latest books, eaten at the latest restaurants. If it's true that a man who is tired of London is tired of life, then I was. At least of that life (I prefer Theroux's observation that a man who is tired of London is tired of looking for a parking space). But coming to Italy was like a renaissance.

K though, still loved it, I think. London, I mean. Her hack buddies were always a merry, boozy bunch compared to the rather stuffy lot of my publishing world. Those were the heydays of Fleet Street, and it was a great place for socialising. If remembrance is now sometimes my companion, as it seems to be as you get older, it's to Wales my thoughts turn, not to London. Maybe I've shut a lot of it away, in a dusty trunk up in the attic as it were. Because you can never really go back, can you?

Increasingly, I don't go anywhere at all. I rarely leave the flat. I venture out to do a spot of shopping but I begin to get panic attacks if I try to venture further afield. I'm happy enough in my fortress. And yet, it feels as if I'm waiting for something. For what, I couldn't tell you.

The crones are still suspicious. Of what, I really couldn't say. Unless they got wind of the fact that I'd decided to kill my wife.

Clapham, Early May

I hate my fucking job. Going out on my bike is what I love doing most now. Aimlessly. Fast. Wind in my hair. Or what bit of it is poking underneath my helmet. Freedom. What I crave.

Other than that, I spend a lot of evenings in my garage. Jo's often busy with work, at the office or at home or away, so there's nothing much to keep me in the house, especially since we lost the boy. I've never been much of a one for TV, unless there's a good doc or film or match on, but I'm picky. Won't just watch something for the sake of it like most people seem to do. Besides, Jo doesn't like me smoking in the house. Neither do I, come to that.

So I can sit in the garage and have a smoke and a scotch or two from the optic I've put up. Well, it's not the garage as such, but an extension I built at the back of it. It's my office cum workshop, (cum cave, Jo says). I feel kind of peaceful here, reflecting on the business of the day if I've been out on a job or two, or admiring my handiwork if I've been working on a bike. I suppose it's my hobby in a way, doing up motorbikes, although I'd never normally use that word to describe it, or list it under hobbies on a form or something. It's just something I do.

I've always been interested in bikes, ever since I was a little kid. I got my first one when I was eighteen and have had at least one on the go ever since – sometimes as many as five. It useful to have one for work, to get to stories quickly, although these days a lot of the stuff I do is not really news at all. The red top tabloids are just interested in chasing so-called celebrities, and that's where I get most of my work. Most of the time I've never heard of the people they send me out to snap - they may have appeared on Big Brother or something - so I have no interest in whatever aspect of their private life is supposedly making the news. Low life, most of them are. I suspect most of the readers really feel the same way. But if the tiniest, tackiest detail appears in print, people seem to think it's worth knowing. Personally I get bored with that degree of revelation even from my nearest and dearest.

Most people think the life of a freelance tabloid photographer is glamorous. It's not, ninety-five per cent of the time. I do like working with reporters on a good story - nailing a crim, scammer or kiddie-fiddler, say. But these days it's all so-called celebrities - most of them way down the alphabet.

And then there's the Editor's stories. That means, 'We don't care how you do it, just get it.' A colleague of mine was sent out to get a pic of a 12 year-old drug dealer who used to hang around the school gates. They couldn't stand it up so he used his son to pose - he was well up for it. They pixelated his face, of course. But his ex got wind of it and rang up the editor to complain. He got the sack. Bloody hypocrites.

It's not without its moments. Not so long ago we were sent down to George Best's house one Sunday evening. We'd had a tip of that he'd been drinking in his local all day - he was supposed to be off the booze - and ended up in a fight. We were nervous about knocking on his door, but he answered it and said he supposed we'd better come in. He was a bit shame-faced about it, but told us the whole thing. It turned out he thought we were cops. It was only when I got my camera out that he twigged and started to turn nasty. By then we'd got the story and the pix, and just legged it. But most of the time - crap.

So a lot of the time now I spend doorstepping someone I couldn't care less about. Sometimes when I get a job I have to flick through those mags Jo gets to see what they look like. You can't really doorstep on a bike because you might have to spend hours outside someone's house, unobserved if possible. Instead I sit in my car discreetly parked a few doors down the street in Primrose Hill or wherever for mind and bum numbing hours. I just have to make sure my lens is focused on the door, to catch them if they go in or out.

I read mostly, although it's hard to concentrate with one eye on a door. It seems to surprise people that I love reading. I like bookshops.

I have to pee in the car. I carry an old pickle jar for the purpose. I've got those little mesh sunshades on the side windows to give me some privacy and hide me when I'm taking pix or wiring them in to the office on my laptop.

I've thought about giving it all up and doing weddings. You can make quite a decent living out of weddings. But then I stick to what I know. Even though I hate it, and find it degrading, I can't seem to break away from it. If only more people bought newspapers with news in them.

So these days I get more satisfaction doing the bikes than I do from work. I started doing them up for pleasure a few years ago and can make a bit of pocket money from them. It's been a lot easier with ebay. You can get almost all the parts you need if you're patient.

The first one I did up was a Honda CX 500 that I bought from a bloke in Guildford. It wasn't in bad nick, but very rusted. I got it for a couple of hundred quid and brought it home in the back of the car after I'd taken the seat out.

It was a bit daunting at first, even though I reckoned I knew what I was doing. I knew about engines and had done quite a bit of painting in my time. I trained in electronics so the wiring was a doddle.

I dismantled the whole thing and laid it out in parts around the garage. I made a note of everything that was in good order and everything that was not. I'd need a new fork for the front suspension, for example, but I thought that would be fairly easy to come by. The frame was rusted, but solid enough. It's almost impossible to find just a frame, even on ebay. The headlamp was in quite good condition too, another very important part.

I set about sanding the whole thing down to the metal. You can get sandblasters but for some reason I wanted to do the whole thing myself with sandpaper. The hard way, I suppose you would call it. I'm a bit of a perfectionist like that. Part of my stubborn streak.

It's the worst part, sanding down. It's a thankless task with not much to show for hours of work and it all looks pretty sad at that point. It feels as if you're going the wrong way. I did all the preparations, filling in with a plastic resin and undercoating.

Then came the best part, the painting. I hung up all the individual sections from the garage rafters and sprayed them each two or three times. Again, I could have taken them all to a garage, but wanted to do as much as possible myself as cheaply as possible. I found the paint code on the internet. It's vital you get an exact match of the original, otherwise it loses value. I got it from a specialist supplier over in Wandsworth. I sanded down finely after each coat and finished off with a lacquer.

As soon as I'd done the petrol tank, a fly smashed smack into the middle of it. I heard the fucker buzzing round and could have put money on it to land on the most prominent part. I'd tried to swat it but was afraid of smashing something else up, so failed. Fucking annoying.

I made the mistake of trying to pick it off with a pair of tweezers. It made one hell of a mess, and I had to begin the whole process again, stripping it down to the metal. The lesson here is that if a fly or something lands on wet paint you let it dry, even though it goes against your instincts. Then you can cut it out and repair the little patch. You'll always know yourself where it is, of course, but no-one else could tell.

I had to get all the chrome done by a metal refinisher. That was one job I knew I couldn't do it myself.

The re-assembly is both rewarding and frustrating. There's always some little piece that's missing, or won't fit. Then it's back to the internet. There are times when you think you'll never be able to do it, you'll never get this old thing on the road. It's like this every time. Patience and perseverance is what it takes.

When I finally finished that old Honda, I got a feeling of elation I'd never quite experienced before. I took her out for a test run and it went like a dream and looked liked a million dollars. It wasn't just a sense of achievement, but also of independence and freedom. Something all my own. The next weekend I took Jo down to the Surrey Hills on the back. I don't think she quite got the same kick out of it as I had, but she enjoyed it.

I hung on to it for a few months to get some pleasure out of it, and then sold it, making a couple of hundred quid on the whole deal. Not a fortune, but it could go towards the next bike. I'd got the bug now. Almost nothing gave me as much satisfaction.

I stuck to Hondas for a while, then branched out into BMWs. But now I need a new challenge. I just have to find out what it is. Perhaps I'm spending too much time in my garage. Jo jokes that my bikes are my friends now.

I've never been a really sociable sort. I know I can be a grumpy sod. And when Dylan was killed, I probably turned in on myself even more. Never been much good at talking, and me and Jo hardly ever talk about him now. Sometimes I catch her staring out of the window, with that empty, dead look. But then when she sees me she'll snap out of it and become her usual self, encouraging and supporting. I don't know where I'd be without her. She's a saint, for putting up with me if nothing else.

She gave me this book, *Men Are From Mars, Women Are From Venus*. In the general run of things, I hate these psychobabble, preachy self-help books. Why should you have to try to fit your life around other people's slogans? You have to figure it out for yourself, don't you? Isn't that what it's all about?

But I did learn something from this book. When a woman is moaning to you, about something that's gone wrong at work, say, she doesn't expect you to fix it. You just have to listen. And I'm better at listening than talking.

She also gave me this diary to relieve the boredom when I'm on a doorstep. People think that being a freelance photographer for a tabloid is glamorous - they're always asking me which celebs I've taken. It's a question I dread, because I hate talking about it. The diary does help me to get things off my chest, I suppose. Jo's way of keeping me as calm as possible.

It's true that since the Old Git turned against me, I haven't had any close friends. That's how I think of Griff now - the Old Git. And it's what Jo means when she jokes about my bikes. God - I hope she *is* joking.

Gradoli, Late May

As K's health first began to fail, when we were still in London, our thoughts turned to Italy, particularly to the Lago di Bolsena where we'd spent a couple of marvellous holidays, our honeymoon even. We'd go there while K got better, we decided. There wasn't much to keep us in London. Or me anyway. K had lots of friends. I seemed to have managed to get rid of most of mine. But it was K that needed to get away.

By then she'd had to give up working, and was past regret. I took an open-ended sabbatical, but they agreed to send some manuscripts for me to work on. It was quite easy to arrange - they were going to have to shed staff, Caroline said, so they would be pleased to pay me piecework. They knew what I was good at - travel, geography, biography. I felt for the shreddable staff, but we'd need some money coming in.

We rented out the Clapham flat to a couple from Edinburgh who'd both got media jobs in London. On the internet we found an apartment to let in Bolsena. The rent was more than we'd bargained for, but it had high ceilings and long windows looking over the lake, and we couldn't resist it.

They were a kind of idyll, those first days here, even with the worry of K's health hanging over us like a hovering storm cloud at the edge of the horizon on a summer's day when you're having a picnic. It was the only cloud really, but little by little we realised that it wouldn't go away, that in fact it was almost imperceptibly moving our way. K wasn't going to get better. The cancer had taken too much of a hold.

K was stoic about it and wanted the minimum of fuss, to the point that it was almost business as usual. She didn't dodge the issues as they came up, but she certainly didn't dwell on them either. She decided not to tell Alex and Jake. She didn't see the point. And was firm about it.

But she did ask me one thing - a hard thing.

'If I get to the point when I can't go on, I want you to put a pillow over my head and kneel on it till I've breathed my last.'

'I can't do that.'

'Yes, you can, Griff. You're the only person who can. You can do it because you love me, and I love you. I don't want to suffer, I don't want you to suffer, and I don't want to see you suffering because I'm suffering.'

She signed up for Dignitas in Switzerland.

'Well, if the time comes, I'll come with you,' I said.

'Don't be idiotic. You'll still have your life to live. Why would you do away with yourself because I'm sick? And anyway, they wouldn't take you. There's nothing wrong with you.'

'I meant I'll come to Switzerland with you, not to the afterlife.'

We had a good laugh about that, but she quickly switched to serious again.

'Griff, I want you to promise.'

'I don't have any choice, do I?'

'No.'

'But how will I know? When you're ready to go?'

'We'll have a code word. It has to be a simple one, because I'll be very weak. But not an everyday one, in case you get it wrong.'

'What then?'

She didn't have to think about it. She'd clearly worked this all out in advance.

'Ox. When does that word crop up in normal conversation?'

'How will I do it?'

'That's up to you. I don't want to know.'

'And what if you're too weak to speak?'

'You'll see it in my pleading eyes.'

So I committed myself to killing her. I supported it in principle, of course - no objections on religious grounds. But a part of me wondered why someone would want to end it all at the lowest point in their life. What about hope? A second chance? Remarkable things can happen. I didn't voice any of this, though. She'd made up her mind and it would just be cruel. I said yes straightaway. I just didn't know if I'd have the courage to carry it through. I did object, however, to her determination not to tell our children. Surely they had a right to know?

'What's the point?' she shrugged.

I thought I could see a point. Jake would surely come over from London more often and even Alex might finally come over from Australia to see her mother before....

But K was adamant.

'I don't want people sobbing over me,' she said when I tried to discuss it. 'You have to take life as it comes and not try to create something artificial - all emotional because I'm going to disappear. And why worry them? It could go on for years,' and she shuddered at the thought.

We went to see specialists in Viterbo, then down to Rome. We were treated very well - appointments were quick and easy and it was all on our EU health card. But there was nothing to be done. The one in Rome did suggest that we return to England where palliative care and the support of our nearest and dearest would help as time went on.

Almost without talking about it or even thinking about it very much we came to see that we would not be going back to London. Neither of us had any family to speak of, apart from the kids. For K, staying in Italy would avoid a lot of dreaded explanation and sympathy, however well-meaning it was.

'I just want a bit of peace,' she'd say.

'What about your friends?' I asked.

'That was then. They were there for the good times. So was I. It's different now.'

I knew what she meant. I wouldn't miss the city I once thought I loved. It's hard to love brick and stone for too long. But we soon realised we wouldn't be able to stay in the beautiful Bolsena flat for very long, or buy one there. Prices were too high. I got a pay-off from work when I left, would continue to work on manuscripts and we had the income from our place in Clapham. But we had the future to think of, and possibly some care for K.

We started looking around for a small flat to buy, outside Bolsena with its vibrant home holiday market. We looked a bit further around the lake. Then a bit further. And we stumbled on Gradoli. It was so much cheaper. You'd get a small flat for what a Londoner might pay for a parking space. In a way you could see why. It was hidden away, in a cleft of a hill tumbling down to the lake, and had nothing particularly to recommend it. No vine-covered terrace restaurants, no postcard views. Yet there was something so quintessentially, well, Italian about it. We kind of took to it.

But we didn't find what we were looking for straightaway. In fact we'd almost given up when we came across this old *palazzo*. It looked almost derelict from the outside (still does) and certainly didn't live up to its name. We almost turned straight around when we drove through the archway, but something made us want to have a look. Idle curiosity, probably. Who lived here? Who would want to?

The plain old building surrounded a lawn on three sides. On the fourth side was a kind of balustrade overlooking the valley below and the lake beyond. Even though you entered the place from the street, it was in fact built on a rocky outcrop high above the valley which sloped down to the lake. We'd read in guide books that in the days when infighting was the norm around here, the gentry used to build these fortified mansions on such outcrops for fear of attack. Gradually they realised no-one was particularly interested in attacking them anymore and normal towns grew up around them.

The two wings on the ground floor were made up of arched doorways which must once have been the stables. Now they seemed to be a mix of garages, workshops and storerooms with a mishmash of doors: wood, corrugated iron, mesh. The plaster had crumbled from the walls here and there and had been repaired with a patchwork of materials and colours.

We met the estate agent there as arranged just before lunch. She was rather a severe looking woman in her thirties in a black suit. Her hair was pulled back in a tight twirl which gave her a look of perpetual surprise, and not pleasant surprise either.

Even she seemed to have little interest in the flat. But we were drawn inside, through one of the doors in the eastern wing, K leading the way. She always loved old places which had an air of mystery about them. We almost had to drag the estate agent with us. We stepped through a small wooden door set in a larger one into a dark stone hallway. After a bit of fumbling we found the light switch, one of those push-in affairs on a timer. There were a couple of staircases leading off in different directions, one frontish-looking door at the back and one to the right.

The flat we'd come to see was on the third floor, under the eaves apparently. We climbed the first staircase and came out on a small landing with another front door to the left and a corridor leading off it to the right. There was no sign of a staircase, so we made our way along the corridor, past a couple more doors until we came to some steps twisting up. Nothing was symmetrical. Even The Surprised One seemed unsure of the way, and I began to suspect she'd never set foot in the building. We didn't see anyone, but I had the feeling that there were people who were aware of our presence, scuttling out of sight as we approached. A couple of the doors were open behind beaded curtains, and delicious smells of home-made cooking wafted out.

We climbed the steps and came onto another small landing, with two doors facing each other. No passages or staircases. The Surprised One produced keys efficiently from her big leather bag and opened the wooden door with a frosted-glass porthole.

It opened into a small vestibule and then into a roomy lounge with a huge Gothic-style fireplace, French windows giving on to a small balcony on the left looking onto the lawn in the *piazza* below and a low window overlooking a tangle of oddly-angled roofs on the right. And on the other side, when we opened the shutters, that magnificent view of the shimmering lake. I could tell K was sold right there and then.

Opening out of this, through an arch on the right, was the world's tiniest kitchen, with a sink, a fridge, a little cooker running of a gas bottle and one cupboard on the wall.

On the left of the fireplace was a door to the main bedroom, going off at a funny angle as it turned the corner of the building. To the right of the fireplace a little hallway up a couple of steps housed two more doors. Behind one was a smaller bedroom and this in turn led to a kind of sun room through French windows. Behind the other door was an old-fashioned bathroom with a rusting bath on iron paws.

There was no ornament or clutter, but some basic old clunky furniture; iron bedsteads, huge sideboard and table, sofas and chairs covered in sheets. The rooms reached up to the roof lined with whitewashed wooden boards. On the floor throughout there was lino whose pattern had worn away. The faded wash on the walls was pealing here and there. It looked as if it had been empty for some time, or used as a holiday home.

The three of us shuffled through the place in almost total silence. It didn't take very long, but there was a feeling of space. The Surprised One made no attempt to point out any virtues or even disguise the fact that she found it all pretty awful. K and I raised quizzical eyebrows at each other now and again.

'Is the furniture included?' I asked.

'I think, yes,' said the Surprised One's voice, while her look said 'Why the hell are you asking me? And why the hell would you want it?'

It was only later when K and I were talking it over back in the Bolsena flat that we discovered we were both......well, in love with it would be overstating the case. Strangely drawn to it, expresses it better. But we'd held off declaring this to each other for fear of appearing to have lost some marbles. It was K who banged her fist on the table and made the decision.

'What the hell!' she said. 'Let's do it.'

It would take a lot of work. But we were up for it. It was ridiculously cheap, so we could spend money on doing it up as we wanted, and have some left over. K broached the subject of whether she was up to it, and whether she'd see it out. She just wanted clarity she said. She could sit at home and not do anything for months, years even. You hear of these cases. Or she could do something that would absorb her. And this flat in Gradoli was it.

Once we'd made up our minds and bought it, things happened remarkably quickly as they can in Italy once you find the right person. We found none of the laziness or inefficiency that others had warned us about.

We had the floor tiled in black marble throughout, a swanky new bath and shower room fitted, the walls re-plastered and whitewashed, and smart green shutters to replace the rotting wooden ones.

And so here I am, sitting on the balcony, serene enough in my demi-paradise. Yet somewhere at the back of my mind there's a niggle that I'm simply marking time, that my life doesn't have much purpose. It's almost as if I'm waiting for something. Oh, and the shower's packed in. There's always something. Life never quite coasts along as you dream it one day will.

Clapham, Late May

Now I'll tackle just about anything in the bike department. I've got three in the garage at this minute. But my out and out favourite is a 1950s Norton 500cc. I'd long wanted a vintage British bike. It's a new departure for me.

I spent ages looking for one. Nothing much on ebay. I found the Norton Owners' Club website but there were more people wanting them than selling them.

In the end I chanced on an ad in a Loot I was reading on the loo. It was in a list of assorted gardening tools and appliances. Probably part of a house clearance. I rang the number and an impatient, gruff guy answered. I asked a couple of questions about the bike but he didn't seem to know much about it. I asked if I could see it. He said OK, as if to say it was no skin off his nose. I arranged to meet him at a house in Golders Green the next evening. I was getting kind of excited and nervous.

I found the house in a street of well-kept semis, apart from number 43 that is. It seemed stuck in the sixties. It had clearly been well cared for at one time but then allowed to run to seed.

I pushed my way up the front path, swatting aside the thigh-high grasses. Beside the door there was a weather-beaten wooden plaque bearing the name Badgers' Croft. I rang the ding-dong bell and a bearded elderly man in black-rimmed glasses opened it straightaway as if he'd been standing the other side, waiting.

'You come about the bike?' he demanded without preliminaries. I nodded.

'This way.'

He took me down the side passage to the jungle of the back garden. We negotiated the half-hidden path to the tumbledown shed at the bottom. Again I could see evidence of love in the past. The lawns were wild with grass but had once been square. Beds in the middle were a tangle of roses and weeds, and the borders dense with all manner of shrubs grown into odd shapes. It was all surrounded by a box hedge sprouting in all directions.

The shed was covered in ivy. It was tilting slightly to one side, as if it had had a fainting spell, and most of the panes were broken and replaced with cobwebs. Yet I could somehow see it when it was neat and creosoted.

The grump got a huge bunch of keys out of his trouser pocket and started fumbling with the padlock. I looked back up at the house. Large handrails led down from the kitchen steps and along the path. It didn't look occupied.

'Is this your place?' I asked, just to make conversation.

'My mother-in-law's,' he said. 'She died.'

'My condolences.'

I could have sworn he gave a kind of snort under his breath. I imagined the rails being added as she grew more and more frail to get her out into the garden she loved. I wondered why her son-in-law or daughter hadn't come round to do the odd spot of weeding or mowing. I didn't like him. He was surly, as if I was wasting his time or asking him a favour.

The bike was on its side in the shed under a whole pile of rubbish. He kicked some of the rubbish away and nodded down to it without a word. In truth it didn't look up to much, but I could tell straightaway it was worth salvaging.

'Is there a log book with it?' I asked casually.

It's always a massive plus if you get the log book with these old bikes – a real selling point. It gives all the bike's specifications, when it was first registered, how many owners it's had etc. It would help me a lot in the renovation. It was a long shot, but then again this seemed the kind of household which preserves things.

For a moment he peered at me aggressively through his thick lenses as if he didn't know what I was talking about. But he suddenly spun round on the spot - so suddenly that he almost made me jump – and started rummaging round in one of the drawers of an old sideboard. After a while he produced a tattered, buff-coloured log book and held it up like a magician pulling something unexpected out of a hat.

I took it and thumbed through it, feeling excited but trying not to look very interested. It had only ever had one owner.

'Was it your father-in-law's? Can you remember him riding it?'

'How much will you give me for it?'

OK, forget the small talk.

'Fifty.'

He could probably get five times that much for it.

'I'll take a hundred.'

'Fifty's all it's worth. Cash'

He puckered up his mouth as if to argue but suddenly seemed to lose all interest.

'When can you pick up it?'

'I can take it now if you can help me wheel it to the car.'

I didn't feel the slightest bit guilty taking it from him at this price. He was a nasty piece of work, and at least the bike would be going to a good home. He didn't give a damn about that, I could tell.

And now here it is, gleaming black in my garage. It was easier to do than modern bikes in some ways and harder in others. There were no complicated electronics. The parts that needed replacing I could generally get from the Norton Owners' Club – at a price. But they gave good advice too.

The other parts could simply be repaired, bashed out by a specialist in old British bikes if necessary, whereas their modern counterparts would have built-in obsolescence. The front mudguard for example needed a hell of a lot of work to get just right. But it was worth it. You must preserve the original if at all possible.

Once I got in with the Owners' Club, it was much easier. Word of mouth helped me get what I needed, such as the tank badge. When it came to the paint, the original specification was in the log book, and I had it made up. I've had enough practice by now to know how to get the best end result. I put all my loving care into it, finishing it to perfection.

I've just taken it out for the afternoon – Easter Monday. I asked Jo to come but she wanted to be out in the garden. It goes like a bomb. A bit of a noisy bomb, but she's got a good throttle on her. I headed for the Surrey Hills.

It was a glorious day, the first time I noticed summer really was coming. There was something old fashioned about the whole trip – the quiet London streets, the heat haze, the evocative roar of the old engine. I passed the Wimbledon Pony Club out in force – all tweeds and jodhpurs – and that only added to the sense of a bygone age.

 I left the A3 just after Guildford and before long I was going down winding lanes, past white wooden signposts on village greens, cricket pavilions, half-tiled cottages with ivy round the porch. The kind of England propaganda films told you England fought the war for. It was far away from the Black Country where I grew up. It didn't really feel like my England. Alien. But I had that fleeting sensation of freedom again. I felt as if I had to get away, right away from the jobs that were driving me nuts.

Since I got back I've been sitting here in the garage with a fag and a scotch admiring my handiwork. Jo comes in just now to have a look. She does take an interest in the bikes but she has her limits, and doesn't indulge me more than she should. For the most part she tolerates it. But the Norton seems to intrigue her more than most. When I was talking about getting one, she told me she thought her grandfather had one when he was younger. She couldn't remember it but had seen photos.

She perches on the desk by the back window. She's got a scarf round her neck and her hands round a cup of coffee. It's chilly now, despite the summery feel of the day.

'Very nice,' she says appreciatively, nodding her head. She gets up and goes across and strokes it, as I have done many times. She sits on it. After a while she thinks it's a good idea to change the subject, now that I'm in a good mood, relaxed.

'I have to go away for work in a month or so.'

She knows I won't like this.

'Where?'

'New York.'

She knows I don't like New York.

'How long for this time?'

'A couple of weeks,' she says with a slight grimace, as if she'd do anything rather than go. She knows the long stays are the worst for me. 'Or so.'

I can't help it, but I always get grumpy when she goes away. And this time, it's longer than the usual four or five days. I know she's been working on a project that's coming to a head. I know it's important to her to go and she wants to. I take a deep breath, trying to stay relaxed, but it probably comes out as a sigh.

'I've been thinking though,' she says, looking at me looking out of the window, 'that you could come over for a few days this time. On me. The middle weekend maybe. We could get out and see things. Do things.'

I know straightaway I don't want to go. She won't really mind me not going. She just doesn't want me to resent her going.

'You've been working really hard lately, David,' she continues. 'You deserve some time off.'

'In fact I was just thinking today when I was out on the bike that I should take some time off,' I say, coming to a decision.

'Oh yeah?' she says sharply, the look of surprise on her face not entirely one of delight.

'But you know I hate New York.'

'Well, I'm sorry, but that's where I have to go. Maybe we could get out of there for a few days. Up to the Catskills. Or Cape Cod.'

'Or I could take the bike and go off somewhere for a week or two.'

Usually I'm wary of taking off more than a week at a time. Work can dry up pretty quickly when you're a freelance out of sight and mind. Do I detect a slight look of relief on her face now?

'The BMW?'

'No, the Norton.'

She looks down at the bike as if it had suddenly given her a shock.

'But there isn't anywhere to put anything. Whatcha call em? Paniers. Your luggage or.......' Her sentence trails off.

'I could just strap a little tent to the back, take a change of clothing, and head off. A road trip.'

'On your own?'

'Why not?'

'Is the bike up to it?'

'We'll soon see.'
'But where will you go?'
Good question. Where will I go?

Gradoli, early June

I am a bit of a recluse now, I must admit. Don't even have a house phone or the internet. I can catch up on emails on the PC which is available to the public in the local library in the afternoons between 3pm and 5pm, if you're lucky. Most evenings I watch classic Italian films on DVD. I'm particularly drawn, I have to confess, to those busty, voluptuous older women dressed in hugging red or diaphanous white, who arouse urges in young lads: Gradisca in *Amarcord* (I Remember), or Sagharina in *8 1/2*. Fellini is my favourite - and Sophia Loren.

But I don't mind. In fact I like it. Everything seems so much quieter and slower here, even though it's little more than an hour away from Rome. You can pop out into the village and get most things done on the spot, if your needs are simple, and mine are.

So why did I get like this? For a while before we left London I'd begun to think I was not for this world of new technology. I coped well enough with it at work, although we still asked for manuscripts to be sent in as hard copies – zip files not welcome. More and more we had to depend on an online world, and what a frustrating world it was, of product key numbers, call centres and drop-down boxes. It seemed to me to strip you of all personality, reduce you to a cog in a dreadful Kafkaesque machine. I used to try to remember what we did before we were swamped with emails. Well, there were phone-calls, meetings, memos. People would come into your office to see you about something, and it could be sorted with in minutes. It doesn't sound that exciting, but there was more variety. Now there are these endless email swirls with people hitting the 'reply all' button needlessly so you got swamped. The more senior you became, the more time you spent deleting emails. It was a Sisyphean task..

I remember one form I had to fill in required you to check your title from a drop-down box. No longer the simple Mr, Mrs, Miss or Ms. It had dozens of the damn things, ranging from Rabbi to President. I'm sure rabbis and presidents are capable of typing in their titles. Another bout of mindless scrolling. The simplest things could take all afternoon. I remember having to enter a 28-digit number for something. If you gave a number to the entire population of the world, it would only require ten digits. It all bored me beyond words.

I'd have short bursts of enthusiasm, thinking I was getting on top of it. I ordered broadband and set out to install it myself. For once the manual seemed relatively straightforward and even well-written in a racy, step-by-step way.

But my heart sank when I came to the words 'This is the easy bit.' Inevitably, it was the most confusing, setting up the wireless connection. The wording and symbol in the manual did not match those on the devices. Three hours later, largely spent on the phone to the so-called helpline, I managed it.

I bought a new laptop and printer and was feeling rather pleased with myself when it all worked. But a couple of weeks later the printer refused to print out a one-page letter. After another thorough and dispiriting read of the turgid manual (doesn't anyone who knows what they're talking about ever edit these things?) I thought I knew what to do. I followed all the steps and lo and behold the OK light came on.

I felt a surge of elation. But when I pressed the OK button nothing happened. The printer had lied to me. It was not OK. It was far from OK. I thought it was my friend, but from now on we were sworn enemies. This time I had to enter a chat room to find the solution. After pages of dialogue (if that's the right word) and having to repeat the whole process to three different people, the printer was forced to concede and print the bloody page.

But it got its revenge in little ways, refusing to work when I needed to dash off a letter and catch the last post. It felt like a battle, and one I couldn't win. I used to get dizzy with frustration, and there were moments when I feared I was about to go mad, have some kind of breakdown and have to be locked away. I took to shouting at my laptop as if it were a friend who'd betrayed you. You should have heard the language. Bluetooth, Blackberry, Redgodknowswhat: every innovation was an irritating must-avoid for me, and I felt out of step with the modern world.

Many of my friends on the other hand could barely tear themselves away from their screens, much to the annoyance of their wives or girlfriends (it did seem to afflict males rather than females). Everything had to be done online.

For twenty years or so I enjoyed a monthly poker evening at a friend's house. After a few hands we'd order a curry from a restaurant down the street and go on playing until they delivered. We'd just choose from a menu he kept for the purpose. Then came the night it was decided to order online from the same restaurant, as it would be easier and quicker. This took at least 45 minutes, and the meal arrived another two hours after that.

Then there was the time we went to a dinner party. One of the guests had to cry off at the last minute with a stomach bug. So they put a laptop at the end of the table and hooked her up to a webcam. It was kind of fun in a way, but I did have to wonder what the world was coming to. Sometimes I think I'm living in the wrong time.

It was such a relief arriving in Gradoli, strolling out to the post office or bank to do your business, stopping for an ice-cream or drink in the main square on the way back, nodding to acquaintances. Even posting a letter could be a pleasure, give you a small sense of achievement. I suppose I had more time on my hands now.

It was harder to escape the dreaded reality TV, but we didn't watch much TV anyway and when we did we could at least derive some benefit from it – practising the language or better understanding the Italian character in that way that even the tiniest, most ordinary things are interesting when you're in a new country.

We loved our flat. As soon as we moved in it felt like home, as if we belonged. In those early days we had our routines. We'd do chores and shopping in the morning. Then after a simple early lunch we'd go out for a drive. From here Rome, Siena, Florence and Orvieto are all doable in a day, and the sea is half an hour away. We bought a little Fiat Punto which did us fine.

Our favourite, apart from The Dying City, became Pitigliano, a clifftop town lying on the border between Tuscany and Lazio. Smaller and less showy than Orvieto, say, it's off the tourist track but just as spectacular in its way.

Houses cling to the cliff for dear life. From across the valley it's hard to tell where the houses stop and the caves below begin. And once you've wound your hairpin way up into the town itself, it's like some fantastic Shakespeare film set, all balustrades and balconies, turrets and towers, angles and arches, corners and colonnades. Steps and ramps in all shapes and sizes run up from little squares at every turn.

Grand carved wooden doors stand alongside rickety little stable doors. No two buildings are the same, nowhere is there any symmetry yet there's a harmony, a wholeness about the place, derived in part by the ubiquitous green shutters which it seems have been fitted to every window by town ordinance. Yet no such harmony could have been planned. It had to grow organically.

The houses are all of stone, unpainted on the whole apart from a daub of pink or mustard wash here and there.

The townsfolk when we first discovered it seemed from another time, although things have changed a little now. They'd stroll down the narrow lanes, the women in old floral dresses and purple cardigans like my grandmother used to wear, the men with sunglasses and walking sticks. They'd blithely ignore the little three-wheeler trucks which would whizz up behind them honking madly.

Women would lower baskets on a string from the upper floors so their neighbours could deposit whatever commissions they'd picked up for them at the store, bellowing at each other during the entire operation.

The men too would be engaged in a loud-hailing debate as if about the very future of the planet. When we got a bit better at the language we realised it would be about a local football match or the latest scandal at the town hall.

So the place had its own small scale bustle, even then. But when you were least expecting it you'd turn a sharp corner in one of the steep lanes and give a start at a fantastic panorama stretching before your feet with just a low wall separating you from the ravine below.

Down there in the valley were the Etruscan ways, for which K developed a particular passion. Secret passageways, underground tunnels – she loved anything like that. The Etruscan ways were the narrow paths carved out of the soft tufa rock on the valley floor. They were used for funeral processions and rituals, like the *torciata* or parade of flaming torches held every spring to banish winter and celebrate renewal, rebirth. While K was still up to it we'd walk along those paths, which wound round the bottom of the cliffs.

The Etruscans fascinated K. They'd lived here in the region for centuries until the Romans wiped them out, but not before they put up a tough, David-and-Goliath fight. There are Etruscan ruins at Vulci, between Gradioli and the sea, and a Museum at Viterbo.

D H Lawrence was another one captivated by them, at a time when much less was known about them. He explored the area in the 1920s and clearly thought they were far more interesting than the Romans, whom he describes as the Prussians of the ancient world.

We visited all these places when we first got here. We'd drive around in the Fiat Punto, listening to Italian pop. K took a particular shine to Gianna Nanini, a fifty-year-old rock star who looks about twenty and has one of those husky, croaky voices that the Italians seem to specialise in. K especially loved her song *Grazie,* loved it to the end. It became our kind of theme tune, even though for me it was a bit near the knuckle. She thanks her lover for the love they've had: *Grazie di questo amore, senza paura, piu forte di noi* (Thank you for this love, without fear, stronger than both of us). But she gets fed up of the fighting and eventually cries *Vattene adesso!* (Go now'). Of course K was going to leave under different circumstances. The song ends: *Lasciame il tuo silencio, spegni la voce, le luci accese. Gracie.* (Leave me your silence. Turn off your voice. The lights are on. Thank you). And then there's the sound of a kiss.

As K got weaker we went out less and less in the car, and eventually stopped altogether. We couldn't even go for a *passeggiata* in the end. She didn't want to go to a hospital or hospice and we both knew by now there was no question of her travelling to Switzerland, for what she called the Swiss option. She liked to keep up the pretence, and seemed to want to talk about it. It was her last defiant act of independence, I suppose. She wanted to stay at home, discretely observing the goings-on in the *piazza*, or looking out down to the lake. I got in the habit too. She wanted to die at home. And she did.

It didn't take years after all. It was a matter of months after we moved into the Gradoli flat, and the end came quickly. She didn't have to say 'Ox.' We buried her in the cemetery outside the town. Jake came from London for it, but Alex said she couldn't make it over from Australia, for which I've never really forgiven her.

They were both furious they hadn't been told that their mother was going to die. Jake had it out with me after the funeral.

'I had a right to be told,' he shouted at me in my flat. It was late afternoon and the balcony door was open. Some of the crones must have been down in the *piazza*, but it was unusually quiet. They would have known about K's funeral, and about my son coming over. I always think it's remarkable how the grapevine works here, despite linguistic barriers.

'It was your mother's decision,' I said. 'What about her right to see out her final days as she wanted? You didn't come here when she was living, why should you when she was dying. And anyway as I told you, the end came very suddenly, thank God.'

Yes, it was a cheap shot, but I was angry too. He stormed out, even though he was meant to be staying another night. I don't suppose I'll ever see him again.

What we or I would have done without Mrs O, I don't know. Oh, I haven't introduced you to Mrs O yet, have I? And Mrs O needs some introduction.

She started to come in to do a bit of cleaning when K could no longer manage, but ended up doing so much more. Still is. She was born and raised in Gradoli but left after the war when she was 19 to find work in the textile mills of Bradford. She'd only recently returned when we found her. Widowed and retired, she came back to nurse her sick sister Francesca.

She doesn't look particularly Italian. More Eastern European I would have said, with wavy auburn hair. She's not that tall, but looks it somehow. Statuesque. Handsome, more than beautiful but sexy like those older women in the Italian classics.

She has a wonderful, idiomatic and idiosyncratic way of speaking, which is hard to replicate but I'm going to try. Macaroni Yorkshire, she told me her husband had called it. She has a discernible Yorkshire accent, seasoned with rolling Italian 'r's and hand gestures, and old-fashioned phrases like, ''E's worrth a few bob or two,' and 'I 'ad a loovely little corrporration 'ouse' ('oo' as in 'good,' not 'food.' In Welsh it would be a w).

Mrs O (I think I've even forgotten her full name. Something Northern like Ollerinshaw) is a good story-teller, infusing things with her sense of drama and humour. Soon after she came she told us the story of how she ended up in Bradford.

'I' was joost after the war, an' y'know things 'ad gone to pot in Italy. No jobs. No-one 'ad any money.'

Her father was some kind of itinerant carpenter and odd-jobber. After the war, said Mrs O, they were living in a stable. They were a large family, including two 'blue babies' – twins. She told me this as if I should know what blue babies were but I didn't really. It didn't sound very good. They died in infancy.

'So things were very 'arrd. Me Dad was a good man but me mother were terrible. She used to beat us wi' a stick if we didn't go to churrch.'

Mrs O doesn't hold with religion and is particularly scathing about Catholicism – well most of it, anyway. This again is one of the fascinating and alluring contradictions in her character. Just after K had been diagnosed, a friend in the village got us tickets to see the Pope. We thought, why not? It sounds rather grand, but we were among thousands at one of the general audiences he held on Wednesdays in the huge pavilion alongside the Vatican, complete with school groups and a Mexican Mariachi band who burst into exuberant song every time someone from Latin America was mentioned. And in the midst of this party atmosphere, the ailing Jean Paul II had to be wheeled out on to the stage on a throne. Neither K nor I were religious either, but it seemed like a nice thing to do, or at least *some*thing to do.

I remember telling Mrs O this, before I knew her so well, somehow expecting and maybe even desiring her approval.

'Oh, what you want to bother with 'im for?' she said, shaking her head and waving her arms, ready for a good ding-dong.

'Well, part of history and all that,' I said.

'Part of history?'

By now her voice had begun its customary crescendo of pitch and projection that would have done a massed choir proud.

'Part of history? I'll tell you what's part of history. Me mother beating me black and blue because I wouldn't go to churrch!' Emphasis on the church that could beat anything in The Messiah.

'Me a sixteen year old girl who shoulda been thinking about romance an' roses an' violins. Having the crap beat outta me because I wouldn't go to church!' Remarkable how she could hit the top note perfectly every time.

'No wonder I packed me little bag and got on that bus at the post office without telling a soul.'

I couldn't think of anything to say.

'It's all crap, religion,' she said, calm now, in one of her astounding changes of tempo and register. 'Except St Anthony.'

'St Anthony?' I enquired, unsure of my patron saints.

'If you lose summat an' prray to St Anthony, you'll find it.'

'But Mrs O,' I protested, 'how can you reject the entire Catholic faith and just believe in one saint?'

'I'm telling you, it's trrue,' she said, banging her fist on the table. 'The next time you lose summat, just whisper a little prrayer to St Anthony and you'll find it.'

I saw a picture of her being quite a rebel when she was young. Things between her and her mother seemed to have to got worse and worse.

'One day I was walkin' past the Post Office and there was a sign in the window saying, "Do you want to worrk in England? Bus leaves here at 11am on Friday." I didn't 'ave any idea of what England was like at the time. To me, it joost meant worrk.

'So I went 'ome and packed me case there and then. Not that I 'ad much. On the Friday I didn't say a word to a soul. Joost went down to the Post Office and got on the rickety ol' bus. That took us to Rome. Then we go' a train to Milan, then another bus to the coast. It took hours an' hours an' hours.

'We got to Saltaire late at night, in the dark, and we all slep' in a dormitory. An' when I woke up the nex' morning, I opened the curtains an' there was a hill covered in bluebells. I though' I werre in Parradise.'

It struck me that anyone who thought Bradford just after the war was paradise must have come from some deeply unpleasant circumstances.

'Did you speak any English?' I asked. She got up from the table in our tiny kitchen and started peeling spuds. K was more or less bed-ridden by then. Mrs O asked me to chop an onion. We had to dance around each other in our tasks.

'Not a worrd.'

'Did you know anyone in England?'

'Not a soul.'

'So what made you want to leave everything behind?'

'Worrk!' she screeched. 'An' there were nowt much to leave anyhow. We didn't 'ave any money.'

She put her thumb and forefinger together and shook them at me.

'You can't imagine wha' i' were like. We 'ad nowt to eat.'

'And you never looked back?'

'Never!'

I was having trouble peeling the onion. The skin was brittle and came off in pieces smaller than the thumbnail I was using.

'Here, give me that,' said Mrs O, grabbing it from me. 'What you do is cut it in half like this,' giving it an executioner's chop with the big knife she kept so sharp. 'Then the skin slips off like a well-used nightie. See?'

She gave one of her suggestive wiggles.

'I remember when I was first married to Mr O. He liked all his food plain, like you Englishmen did then. Or you Welshmen. Were you the same?'

It's always impressed me that Mrs O makes the distinction between the English and the Welsh in a way that even some native English people don't.

'Worse,' I said. 'They liked it even plainer.'

'Any road, when he came home from the factory, all he'd want was summat like beans on toast. Which suited me fine as I didn't have much time before me night shift. But I used to jazz it up a bit, without him knowing, like. I just used to add a bit of onion first, and then when they started selling garlic in the market, a bit of that. Then some fresh tomatoes. He never cottoned on. But he used to tell his mates I opened the best tin o' beans in England. That's right, just dump em in the pan.'

She grabbed a handful of basil leaves that she'd got growing on the window sill and threw them into the tomatoes and onions she'd got simmering in the local olive oil.

'By heck, I remember an all when they started selling olive oil in the shops. Thought I'd gone to heaven. Before that, they only used to sell it in the chemists' for sickly babies and that. Didn't tell him about that either. He'd have only said not more of your foreign muck or summat like that. But he got the taste for it alright.'

I found this Mrs O's story about leaving on that bus moving, and never tired of asking her for details. They changed over time, of course, getting more dramatic with each instalment. I know that Post Office well now. It's in a little square on the street that runs up off the main road through the town, across the valley from our *palazzo*. I've stood there sometimes, trying to imagine a nineteen year old girl waiting for the ramshackle old bus after the war, clutching a battered leather suitcase. I was almost transported back to those times, so strong was the sense of Mrs O taking a step into the unknown, saying goodbye to all she had ever known.

K came to rely on her more and more. She was down to earth, practical, direct and unsentimental – all the qualities that K needed as she faced the end. Mrs O was nursing her invalid sister too. But she'd sit with K for hours and hours, telling her stories to make her laugh or cry – Mrs O could switch from one to the other in a blink of an eye, so in the end you wouldn't know what the tears were for. Sometimes when K and I could barely move or even speak with the horror of it all, Mrs O would fill in the silences, and we both loved her for it.

She still comes three days a week to do some cleaning and her fantastic cooking. The wonderful thing is that she can cook great British dishes, authentic Italian cuisine, and her own special hybrids, such as potatoes roasted in goose fat sprinkled with the fennel flowers (*finocchio*) you can find in the hedgerows here. And no-one makes better gravy than Mrs O. When K was alive we used to have a traditional roast once in a while.

So Mrs O provides a link to home, to the past. She doesn't subscribe to the throwaway society, and there's a drawer in the kitchen full of neatly-folded brown paper bags, candle ends, and old boxes of matches with only a couple of live ones among all the dead. My mother had a drawer exactly the same. It's the world of Brasso, carbolic soap, coal scuttles and tea-cosies.

Mrs O's sister still needs looking after, and I think Mrs O can do with the money. 'A bit o' pocket money,' is how she puts it. But she also seems to enjoy our chats, and sometimes joins me on the balcony for an *aperitivo* or two as the sun begins to sink.

She finds it difficult in some ways to be back in Italy and seems to yearn for life in Bradford. She misses Radio 4, so I've brought her a small shortwave radio so she can listen to some old favourites on the World Service. She reads a lot and likes to talk about books, what we've read and liked, and she borrows some of mine.

'It's the 'umour I miss the most,' she says, and does have a robust, earthy sense of one herself.

She told me today she was in the Post Office (that same one where she caught the bus all those years ago), in a queue of sorts, when a young woman rushed in and pushed ahead of her. Mrs O protested. The young woman said she had to get back to work.

'So I said, "An' whar' am I goin' to do – sit at 'ome scrratching me fanny all afternoon?"

'Well, the 'ole place went quiet, an' everyone stared.' She opened her eyes wide. 'Me an' me big trrap. Tongues'll be waggin' down there tonight I bet,' and she nodded down to the crones in position on the other side of the piazza.

They did indeed seem to be looking up at us, and clucking. Sometimes I dread to think what they think of us, both outsiders in different ways, although Mrs O rarely stays for supper, let alone the night. Still, it gives them something to talk about, she says. Other times I couldn't give a damn what they think. Funny how it changes.

Mrs O herself is rather scathing about them and their parish pump ways.

'The latest thing they're all complaining about is the Chinese who they think are tekkin' all their jobs,' she says. 'Silly booggers.'

What jobs they are meant to be taking in Gradoli is a bit of a mystery. But they can be quite – well, there's no other word for it – racist here. Mrs O notices it too, after the modern diversity of Bradford. And God knows she was on the receiving end of it herself sometimes when she first moved to England.

K had one of her old journo friends to stay not long after we moved in. He came with his flamboyant, not to say camp, Jamaican boyfriend, Grant. He'd brought his music with him on his iPod or whatever, and managed to rig it up so it would play through our speakers. A favourite of his was *Enjoy Yourself* by Prince Buster. He and his mother used to play it on a scratchy gramophone after Sunday dinner, doing the latest dances. I had a vivid picture of its old jazz strains drifting across the veranda of the house in Jamaica on sunny Sunday afternoons, as indeed it drifted out over our balcony. It became our favourite too, so evocative of those carefree times. We were sure that more than one of the old crones stopped saying *'Buona Sera'* to us for days after that. Ok, they'd probably rarely seen a black guy apart from the Africans who sell handbags and jewellery in the market on Tuesdays. I'd put money on it that they'd never seen one step over their threshold. I told Mrs O about their visit, then I remembered something else.

'While they were here visiting, the woman with the ground floor flat collared me as we were all coming in one night,' I told Mrs O. 'She seemed angry. Our Italian wasn't so good then but we got the gist of it. She was complaining that we were using the hall light. It was one of the push-in affairs. But it came from her electricity bill. But why had she not said anything until then?'

On the top of the stairs leading up from the hall there were indeed about ten different light bulbs hanging from the wall, presumably one for every flat. I'd no idea where the switch to ours was.

'Ohh, don't tek any notice of her,' said Mrs O, drawing on her cigarette.

'I don't. I wondered if she wanted any money and was going to ask but I just couldn't be bothered. So that's why we use the torch.'

'Oh, well. I'd better be wending me way 'ome,' said Mrs O, downing her third glass.

She was no slouch when it came to drinking her fair share.

'If I 'ave any more I'd be tempted to show 'em me knickers as I'm walking past 'em.'

I wouldn't put it past her either.

I went to run myself a hot bath, but the hot tap was reduced to a trickle. Must ask Mrs O about a plumber. The whole place is falling apart. There's always something to be done, something needing attention.

France, early June

Jo watched me suspiciously as I polished the Norton.

'You really going to go then?'

I knew she hadn't believed I would. But I made my mind up. And once I've made my mind up......

'Yes. I told you I was.'

'And where are you going exactly?' she asked, looking at me through the corner of her eyes.

'Across the Channel and see where the fancy takes me.' I really didn't have a plan at that stage.

'It's very unlike you, just to take off like that,' she said.

It was true. I usually liked to have a plan. But I felt the need to get away, and New York wasn't where I wanted to go. Maybe even then there was some unfinished business at the back of my mind, but I wasn't conscious of it, or hadn't put it into words.

'Won't you be lonely?'

'Nah. A change is at good as a rest. It'll be an adventure.'

'Well, I'm glad you're doing something instead of moping around when I'm gone.'

She went into the house and came back with a brown paper package, book-shaped.

'I've bought this for you. A sort of companion.'

Here she was, up to her reforming tricks again. I tore it open, curiosity getting the better of me. *Zen and the Art of Motorcycle Maintenance.* I couldn't help giving a little chuckle. I'd heard about it, of course. But I had no idea if it really was about motorcycle maintenance. I decided not to ask.

'Thanks.'

I dropped her off at Heathrow that afternoon for her flight to New York.

'Well, have a good time,' she said, kissing me goodbye. And then, with a frown and a smile, 'I don't like it when you're secretive.'

I laughed. 'No secrets. I promise you.'

I set off early next morning, a Sunday, with a light tent and sleeping bag and a few clothes strapped to the back.

My toilet bag was a grooming kit in a little leather case Jo had given me a couple of Christmases ago. It had a mini toothbrush and a razor with a screw-on handle. I wondered at the time what on earth it was for, but of course I looked pleased. Well, now I knew. And come to think of it, it wasn't a bad idea since I spent quite a bit of time on the road. I had a Swiss army knife in my pocket for cutting food and opening bottles. And that was it.

It was a glorious day, like the Easter Monday when I first took her out. The empty streets and hazy heat gave everything that still, permanent quality. I left the A3 and retraced my journey as I remembered it up and down the winding lanes of the Surrey Hills. It was all there, down to tiny details like a red brick bungalow glimpsed through pine trees as I took a certain corner. Somehow though I couldn't quite recapture the thrill of that first outing a month or so ago. It's usually pointless to try to recreate the past, I thought. Although somewhere deep down I realised I had an unformed plan to revisit the past on this journey, to visit......

Still, I had a sense of escape, of putting everything behind me. I got on the motorway again and caught the Shuttle at Folkestone. In France I avoided the motorway tolls and took the country routes, down through the straight poplar-lined roads of Picardy.

Just when I was coming into a town called Beauvais the engine started phut-phutting and gradually petered out. Clouds of blue smoke bellowed from the exhaust. It would either be a piston which had gone or an exhaust valve. Either the fuel was not getting in or not getting out. If it was the valve, a garage could fix it in a couple of hours, but a piston would take two or three days as they'd have to order it. In any case there wouldn't be a garage open today, so at best I'd have to wait till tomorrow.

Luckily I was on top of a long hill leading down into the town and so I freewheeled until I came to a garage, as there often is on main roads on the outskirts of towns. It was open for petrol but the repair part was closed. As I wheeled the bike on to the forecourt, the attendant looked up from filling a tank, and shook his head. I kept wheeling it across to the side of the repair shop. He came across crossing his open palms one over the other to indicate the place was closed, I supposed.

I managed to convey that the bike had broken down, and I'd have to leave it there.

'Tomorrow,' he kept saying in English.

It was annoying, because I could have done the job myself if I'd had the tools.

He watched me park the bike and lock it, and take my rucksack and tent. He shrugged, as if to say 'On your own head be it.'

'Camp site?' I asked.

'Camping?' he asked.

I nodded, and he pointed down the road in the direction of the town.

I set out without much hope, but before too long I did indeed come across a small campsite just off the main road. As usual in France, it was well signposted and had good facilities. I put up the tent and took a stroll into the town. It was dominated by an ancient, dirty cathedral but didn't have much to recommend it. Not that I could find. It had a couple of fairly modern-looking squares in the centre. I wondered if it had been bombed in the war. I found a cafe that was open and went in and had steak-frites and two or three beers. No-one took much notice of me. They must have been used to people passing through. I might have relaxed and enjoyed it if I could have stopped myself from worrying about what the morrow would bring. So much for my flying start, the freedom of the open road.

At least I got a good night's sleep after the early start, so I woke ready for action, packed the tent and made my way back. I hadn't realised I was so worried about the bike until I saw it standing where I left it with a huge wave of relief.

It's funny how all garages are the same the world over. As I wheeled it in there wasn't a soul to be seen. A few tools were lying around and a radio playing music somewhere in the back competed with the sound of metal being hammered. It all had an atmosphere of unhurried activity.

'Allo,' I shouted, unsure it was the right thing to say, feeling a bit of a fool. After a few seconds a short stocky guy in blue overalls and a beret appeared, a cheroot dangling from the corner of his mouth. He was wiping his hands on an oily rag, probably making them dirtier.

He looked at me suspiciously as if I was some kind of intruder, thrust his chin towards me and said something in French that sounded vaguely threatening, his cheroot bobbing up and down.

I nodded towards the bike and the only thing I could come up with was, '*Kaput*,' which as soon as I said it thought was probably German, not French. He seemed to understand and to notice the bike for the first time. He bent over to have a look.

He seemed to take an interest in the old bike, because he looked up and smiled. I could tell he admired it. Good job he was an older guy. A younger guy might have dismissed it as a pile of old junk.

He looked over his shoulder and shouted something. I was trying to figure out what – not a hope – when a couple of colleagues sauntered over, wearing the same oily overalls. He must have shouted at them to come and have a look.

There was a lot of bending over, pointing, fiddling, heated discussion, wagging of heads, *ouis* and *nons*. Eventually the bloke in the beret, now on his knees, looked up and smiled as if to say, 'She's going to be alright' like a doctor in a film. I made a circle with the thumb and forefinger of my left and poked in and out of it with my other forefinger. I realised it looked a bit obscene, but it did the trick because they both laughed and nodded. It was the exhaust valve.

He held up three fingers.

'*Trois heures*?' I asked, and he nodded enthusiastically. Then he pointed over at the car they were working on and held up one finger, then pointed over to the bike. They'd finish the car first and then start on the bike.

I went round to the little cafe part of the petrol station and had a couple of coffees and croissants to while away the time. I watched the people coming and going, thinking how the tiniest thing can be interesting when you're in a different country, things you wouldn't notice at home. I took the book out of my bag and started flicking through it. It WAS about motorcycle maintenance, but also about a father on a road trip with his eleven-year old son, with a lot of philosophy thrown in.

'You clever little thing,' I thought. She knew it was a good book for my trip, that I'd have to read it. It started well. I had to admire his attitude to his bike, with an order behind everything. You should see my garage back at home: spanners and screwdrivers arranged in racks on the wall in descending length like a xylophone; jars with screw and bolts and nuts ranked in order; storage organisers for bits and bobs with all the little drawers clearly labelled. Not random tools chucked in a holdall in the attic, like some old friends I could name have.

By the time I'd got back the old mechanic had already taken the top of the engine off. He found the valve and freed it with a couple of gentle taps on a screwdriver with a hammer. Then he cleaned it and greased it and set to putting the top of the engine back on. I was itching to help him but thought it was better to leave him alone. That's the good thing with old models like this. Often you can bash something out on a workbench and don't need spare parts when the least little thing goes wrong, like you do these days.

After he'd finished he stood up and nodded at the ignition. I turned the key and it started up straight away and purred like a kitten. We smiled at each other and I took my wallet out. He only charged me a few euros. He must have really liked the old Norton. I tried to add a few for a tip but he waved it away. An honourable man. We parted the best of mates, shaking hands and nodding and laughing, saying things the other didn't understand.

I made my way slowly through the town, following the *Toutes Directions* signs, which I always think of as particularly useless when you're looking for one, but anyway I got to the other side and followed the signs to Paris. As I started getting nearer I took the opposite direction, veering towards the west. I knew I was probably wiggling around a bit, but I was quite enjoying it and soon signs to Versailles started to appear. I thought I'd just get near enough to see the chateau. I'd always wanted to see it. I came upon it suddenly and rode into the car park. It was really grand, if a bit over the top for my taste. I couldn't imagine why so many people would queue to pay to troop through room after room, although I wouldn't have minded seeing the Hall of Mirrors where the treaty was signed.

It was about six in the evening now and I was getting quite hungry, so I thought I'd call it a day. I'd spotted a camping sign on the way and decided to go back in case I couldn't find another.

I pitched the tent and walked down to a little supermarket and bought some rolls, that holey cheese you see in cartoons, tomatoes, water, and a bottle of plonk in a plastic bottle. All for about five euros.

I had my supper in front of the tent. Then I stretched out under the stars and read my book. The son was fifteen - the same age as Dylan would be now. Perhaps I was meant to face things I haven't really faced all these years. I did imagine him on the back of the bike with me. I would have treated him far better than the guy treated his son, that's for sure. But then he was clearly a bit nuts. All this Phaedrus shit. The wolf. People do say I'm a bit of a lone wolf sometimes.

It was a lovely night, and I was tired. I finished the bottle, at peace with the world. I wondered where I'd head the next day. Something was driving me south, towards what I didn't know, or at least was unwilling to admit it.

I must have fallen asleep on the spot, outside the tent. I woke when the sun came up the next morning, stiff and cold. It was silent at first, apart from a few birds. But soon I heard the sounds of people starting their day, kids playing, and the smell of strong coffee. I took a shower in the small block in the middle of the campsite, and bought a black coffee and croissant from a van nearby.

The guy gave a kind of cross between a little laugh and a snort when I asked for *un cafe noir*. I sat down to drink it and thought about that. Then I remembered you have to ask for *un cafe au lait* if you want milk in it. So maybe they didn't say black coffee, because that was the default. It would sound pretty funny, I could see. Like us asking for a brown tea.

Not far from my tent, half a dozen bikers with GB plates were packing up. They looked like the original hairy bikers, and I recognised them, or at least one of them. I'd exchanged a couple of words with him on the Shuttle. I know it often happens like this on a bike trip – you keep bumping into the same people. Most bikers like it. It gives them a certain camaraderie of the road.

'Watchya, mate,' the Hairy Biker said, coming up to me and giving me a high five. 'Nice kecks.'

He was being friendly, I know, but I didn't particularly want to discuss my trousers with strangers. They weren't anything special anyway, just some Swedish khakis with padded knees. I said this to him and said I must be on my way.

'Where you headed?' he asked.

'Not sure yet.'

'Oh well, maybe see you on the road. We're going south.'

'Yeah, maybe.'

I packed up in a jiffy, and took to the motorway, still happy with my sense of adventure. Maybe I would head South too. It was another cloudless day, and I enjoyed the ride for the most part. Of course there were quite a few long spells on long, straight roads that were pure tedium. At other times though, as the sun broke through trees or bounced off a stream, when I felt as if my life had only just begun.

A few kilometres down the road, I noticed some flashing lights in my mirror. They were motorbikes. I sped up to try to shake them off, but they kept up, and started gaining on me. As they got closer, I recognised the front one as belonging to the guy who'd spoken to me at the campsite. Perhaps they just wanted to be buddies, to ask me to join their group. It was the last thing I wanted. Inevitably they'd ask me what I did, and the conversation would follow its all-too-familiar lines. This cat-and-mouse kept up for some time, but I couldn't quite shake them off, and couldn't keep this up for long - the old girl wouldn't take it. I began to feel uneasy - there was something insistent about the flashing lights and the honking horns.

I was relieved when I saw I service station exit coming up. I took it, but my heart sank when I saw them follow me. For an instant I thought about driving straight through but there was no sense in it. I couldn't win.

So I pulled up in the bike park outside the little cafe and got off. The chasing pack came roaring up, their leader waving something at me as they did so. I still couldn't figure out what they wanted.

He got off too, and came over waving whatever he had in his hand.

'Mate,' he said, 'you left your wallet at the camp site.'

A wave of relief swept over me, but also a degree of foolishness.

'Oh God, thanks. I hadn't even noticed it missing,' I said, taking it from him. I knew it wouldn't go down well if I offered him something, but felt a bit cheap all the same. Honour among bikers, and all that.

'Look, mate. Why don't you hook up with us? We're heading to Aix-en-Provence and then down to Cannes, down France's Grand Canyon. Great biking country. We've got it all mapped out.'

'Well thanks, but I'm heading to Italy to look up an old friend.'

I don't know why I said that. Desperation, I suppose. The Hairy Biker looked crestfallen, and a little offended.

'OK, well come along with us for the ride before you go your merry way.'

'I'm going to head across country a bit, take some pictures.'

'OK.' He wasn't smiling any more. 'But if you change your mind, you'll know where we'll be. You'll find us easily enough.'

He went back to the others waiting on their bikes and said something to them. There was some shoulder-shrugging and they went on their way.

I had a coffee, waiting for them to get far enough ahead. The episode had unsettled me, made be feel lonely. At first I'd loved that feeling of riding off into the sunrise, to destinations unknown. But now it began to strike me that I was aimless. The days were good but the evenings were getting to be a drag, even for a bit of a loner like me. I even began to consider taking up the offer of the Hairy Bikers but dismissed it in the next instant. Didn't want to compare routes or make any vague plans to hook up along the way. I'm used to having my own destinations and deadlines, doing things my own way. Where was I going? What was the point of this trip?

Maybe Jo was right. It would have been better to have done this with a buddy. Except I no longer have a buddy I'd want to go on a road trip with. Perhaps that's why I'd been thinking almost subconsciously of the Old Git, and it was the first thing I said to the Hairy Bikers. He lives somewhere in Northern Italy, doesn't he? If he's still alive. But surely I would have heard somehow if he'd died.

It's been five years – no, more – since we last spoke. Since that night. I wasn't even sure I wanted to see him. But something told me this was the right thing to do, to try to track him down at least. Then this trip would have a point after all. We were such good friends for all those years. We complemented each other in a way. Even though I used to call him a Welsh peasant he was cultured and clever. I suppose I'm more the active type, practical and good with my hands, but deep down I'm a sensitive soul.

Basically I'm quite shy, although people never believe it. I must come across as a bit of a goon. But he drew me out of myself. He did things like take us to the opera, which he loved. I didn't particularly, but I liked going. Made me feel an insider rather than the outsider I was more used to. He wasn't afraid of the things I was afraid of – certain social situations. He was at home anywhere, the proverbial life and soul. So we were a good team, if somewhat of an unlikely pair. K used to call us Tweedledum and Tweedledee. And I suppose he was a bit like the brother I never had.

But what he did to me was nasty. To me he wasn't the same guy after that. It was like I didn't know him all of a sudden after twenty years. He wasn't even like a stranger, because even strangers have possibilities. They have the potential to be your friend.

So what did I want to do if I found him? Confront him? Get an apology? Then what? Did there have to be a then what? As the countryside sped by, I got very angry again, like I used to after it first happened. Yes, I would track him down, and I would confront him. It was a snap decision and sometimes they're not the best ones. They can change your life for good. Or bad. But it felt right.

I tried to remember the name of the place they moved to in Italy. When K died, Jo got the address from somewhere, and wrote him a nice letter. We never heard back. After that even Jo said, 'Fuck him, the Old Git.' I wondered if she'd know the place. She might not have the address on her in New York. She might remember though.

But somehow I didn't want to bring Jo into this. It would make it even more complicated. She might try to dissuade me from my course of action. And now I'd made my decision. I tried to picture Jo's neat writing on the envelope she gave me to post. I think I did clock it at the time. I might even have thought that some good could come of it, that we might be able to patch things up.

I kept searching for the answer as I continued my journey for a couple of hours south. Somehow there was no going back now. I'd have to go on with my mission and face whatever needed to be faced. But the name of the town just wouldn't come to me. I started heading for the Alps to cross into Italy. There'd be some fantastic photos at any rate

I found a campsite just outside a little village, near a river in a gorge. It was only the third night but I'd already got my routine.

Parked the bike and pitched the tent and walked into the village for supplies – bread, salami, cheese and wine. I lay down by the tent and just noticed I'd got a message from Jo.

How u?

Gd. U?

Gd. Whre u?

Alps. U?

NYC. Usual. Things going OK. Whre nxt?

Italy

OK. Hve gd tme. Kp in touch xx

U2 xx

At least I hadn't lied. I never like lying to Jo, although sometimes it's hard not to. But now I was about to deceive her, and maybe would have to lie sooner or later. Oh, well, we'd see how it went.

I downed the last of the wine and snuggled up for another night. I still felt relaxed, but excited at the same time. And just when I stopped racking my brain for that place in Italy, it came to me, as it often does when you stop thinking about it. Bolsena. That's where the Old Git lived. I'd head for Bolsena.

Florence, June 12th

It was Mrs O who suggested the trip to Florence, to see Michelangelo's David.

'I've never seen it,' she said over a second glass on the balcony one evening last week, 'and I've always wanted to.'

Mrs O sometimes struck me as oddly unpatriotic when it came to things Italian, with so many things to be proud of. Of course she'd made her life in England. In many ways she was more English than Italian, and northern English at that. She had a healthy individualism when it came to artiness. She didn't follow the crowd and made up her own mind of what she liked and what she didn't. But it surprised me that she didn't rave about a lot of things in Italy that I did. It was her birthright after all.

I can't say that Michelangelo's David was something I'd always longed to see. You hear so much about it, it becomes just another of those phrases. Same with the Mona Lisa. When I saw it in Paris I was so disappointed. Couldn't see what all the fuss was about.

'Have you seen it?' persisted Mrs O, when I must have fallen quiet for a moment or two.

I could sense she wasn't going to let go.

'No, I can't say as I have.'

'Why don't we mek a day of it? Set out early? They say the queues are always quite long. Then we could have a nice lunch somewhere. I could get me cousin to stay wi' me sister for a day.'

It was clear this was something Mrs O really wanted to do. She didn't ask for much. But as I think I've mentioned, I rarely venture out of the village these days. Don't even get out of the flat very much. I dread the panic attacks, and I'm sure that's what brings them on. I've got my routines, and I feel safe with them. When Mrs O asked about this, I immediately felt nervous, but didn't see how I could refuse. Then I had another thought. What if it was all a ploy to get me out of the house? She sometimes mentioned that I should get out more. Or at least occasionally. Maybe she thought I needed taking in hand, before I became a total recluse. I had to admit, I'd had similar thoughts myself.

So I agreed, full of misgivings. We arranged it for today. Mrs O insisted we set off at eight o'clock in the morning. I was still asleep when she let herself in with her door key and prodded me awake, pulling the covers off my lower half and jabbing at my legs and tickling my feet.

'Come on, let's be 'aving you,' she said in her no- nonsense way. 'The coffee's on and I brought frresh brread. I'll boil an egg for you. You got to get up now.'

'Uh?'

I wasn't yet aware of what she was on about, and certainly wasn't ready to face the day. Then I remembered. David. We were off to see David.

I was sorry I'd agreed to it. I didn't really feel up to it, and turned over, cocooning myself in the duvet. But she dragged it off me and took it into the living room so I couldn't snuggle up again. I staggered out of the bedroom and was revived slightly by the smell of strong coffee. I went to stand in the shower and pressed the button. It was a moment or two before I remembered it didn't work. I turned on the bath taps but now nothing at all came out of the hot tap. I shouted at it, letting out an expletive.

'Wassa marrer?' shouted Mrs O from the kitchen. 'Didn't you get the plumber in yet?'

'Oh yes, he's in here with me now, only he forgot to bring his wrench,' I snapped back.

'Ahh, bugger off,' she said, more to herself than to me, I could tell.

The day was starting badly. I've never been a morning person and was daunted by the day ahead. I had a cold bath and felt a bit better. Then I had a pee and tried to flush the loo, but something seemed to snap inside the cistern and the handle drooped forlornly towards the floor.

'Fuck it, fuck it, fuck it,' I bellowed.

I lifted off the cistern lid and could see that the screw in the siphon had snapped. There was nothing to be done for the time being. I lifted up the flush part and at least that worked.

I reeled into the kitchen, feeling defeated before the day had begun. Mrs O was holding a cup of steaming coffee up for me.

'Look, if you don' want to go, joost say. I can go another time.'

I could tell she was inwardly seething about my behaviour on this day she'd been looking forward to and deserved. She was right. I suddenly felt bad, ashamed at my behaviour.

'No, I'm up now. Let's go. We'll have a nice day.'

Both of us knew I didn't believe it. But I was starting to feel a little more human. We got ready, keeping out of each other's way as much as possible.

I felt the usual panic attack on leaving the flat: dizzy, wobbly, as if the stairs were getting softer and softer and eventually I'd sink through them, and very, very frightened. But I knew that if I kept breathing deeply and regularly, and concentrated on the task in hand, then I wouldn't pass out and nothing bad would happen. Mrs O was familiar with this performance and affected to take no notice, for which I was very grateful.

Mrs O waited by the arch while I brought the car up from the little car park beneath the wall, and she clambered in, with a little difficulty. I felt a little better once we were in the car, and we headed down to the garage on the lakeshore road to fill up on petrol.

As we drove back off up the hill I felt the need to restart the day, but I couldn't think how. Mrs O would have waved away any apology. She didn't hold with them, as she didn't hold with many things.

'Do you know anywhere nice we could have lunch?' I asked.

'Ahh aye, I'll sniff somewhere out.'

We drove through the hills past Siena rather than carry on to the motorway in the valleys between Rome and Florence. I felt more confident on the back roads. These went through the Chianti hills, whence of course the wine gets its name. It was a splendid day, not too hot, and the early morning sun showed the rolling hills off to their best. No tourist brochure could have done justice to that breathtaking Tuscan landscape.

We cheered up considerably, both of us enjoying an almost childish excitement at the prospect of a day out. I hadn't experienced anything like this for a good long time. Mrs O would point out certain places along the way, giving little snippets of history or the origin of a certain wine. We put the bad start behind us.

We came into Florence quite quickly. It's not a big place. I was glad I remembered the way more or less from previous visits. We found a place to park south of the river by the walls of the Pitti Palace, where, Mrs O informed me, wedding masques for the Medicis evolved into the first early operas.

'It's the birthplace of operra,' she said matter-of-factly.

She shares my love of opera. In Wales, as in Italy, it's not the class-ridden thing it is in England. Lots of people love it, and will hum arias while they're waiting at the bus stop. My mother would take us kids to see the Welsh National Opera when a tour came to our town, and we must have inherited it from her. It would play in a huge shed somewhat euphemistically called The Pavilion. My brother and I used to think it used to be an old aircraft hanger during the war, although looking back, I don't see how it could have been. Any plane taking off would have flown into the side of a hill.

My Dad never came with us. 'Come and see the show,' my mother used to say to him. She always used to call it the show, which was ever so slightly embarrassing. 'No, I'm not much of a showman,' my dad would say, which was a bit of a joke as in fact he was a showman. In his parlance, a showman would be someone who took their livestock to compete in agricultural shows.

Mrs O and I headed to the river and pushed our way through the swarming tourists and hawkers on the Ponte Vecchio. I suppose I'd vaguely assumed that the David was in the Uffizi gallery, and my heart sank when I saw the queues outside, but Mrs O swept grandly on through the Piazza della Signoria, gesturing towards the two massive copies of David outside the Palazzio Vecchio.

'Isn't it in the Uffizi then?' I shouted, struggling to keep up with her.

'No, at the Galeria dell' Academia, a bi' further on.'

'Do you know Florence quite well, then?'

'Ahh no. I came 'erre for the firrst time when I came back to Italy.'

'You didn't come as a little girl? It's so near.'

'No. I always wanted to, bu' it costs money to be arty y'know. We neverr 'ad any.'

'Didn't you come on school trips?'

'Oh aye. We 'itched lifts on passing American tanks,' and she laughed her smoker's wheezing laugh.

'So you haven't seen the Uffizi?'

'Aye, that's wherre I went that time I came. I'm not a peasant, y'know.'

'Well, you're the one that always goes on about living in a stable.'

'Ah well, I've come on a bi' since those days, even so.'

There was another long queue outside the Galeria, and when we asked we found there was a wait of about an hour and a half. We were both determined to see what we'd come to see though, and took our places at the back.

In front of us was a group of rather annoying Amercian teenage girls, talking loudly over each other, mainly it seemed about their boyfriend's wardrobes.

'Sometimes Greg wears khaki pants and Guinness T- shirts, and sometimes he wears Guinness T-shirts and khaki pants,' said one, flicking her hair back. The others nodded as if this were a perfectly normal thing to say, and then waded in with their own descriptions.

Mrs O gave them a withering look but of course they were oblivious. She then looked at me and rolled her eyes, as if to say, 'I may be able to stand the heat and the hanging about, but I don't think I could put up with this for an hour and a half.'

'Thank God for Eurrope,' she said out loud.

They went on in the same vein, talking about clothes and boys, each in turn listing what they did or didn't like. Sometimes now I do have a fantasy about going back to London. There's not much to keep me here now, apart from the panic about going outside. But this inane chatter reminded me of how vacuous modern life can be. British youth must undoubtedly be the same. So must the Italians, for that matter. Except it sounds as if they're reciting poetry.

I noticed that it seemed perfectly acceptable for one member of a party to stand in the queue while the others went off for a coffee or something. I suggested Mrs O did the same, and she looked at me gratefully. She was not one to stand on ceremony. She promised to bring me one back and toddled off. We were friends again.

Sure enough it took almost exactly about an hour and a half. Mrs O had stationed herself outside a cafe opposite and came with a coffee about ten minutes before we got in.

It was such a relief to be inside the cool gallery. By tacit agreement we made straight for the David, at the end of the longest wing. You saw it in an alcove as you entered the opposite end looking quite small. But as you walked towards it, it seemed to grow and grow. When you reached it, it towered over you. I never realised it was so colossal, and even the copies in the square didn't prepare you for it.

I could immediately see what all the fuss was about. There was none of that disappointment of seeing an icon that I'd experienced with the Mona Lisa.

'You see the 'ands, 'ow big they are,' whispered Mrs O as we began to circle it like everyone else is doing. She was as awestruck as I was.

'I' was originally meant to be outside on a plinth, like the ones in the Piazza della Signoria. ''Is 'ands were made bigger so they'd look the rright size when you looked up at 'em.'

It was good being there with her. Her knowledge made it somehow even more alive. I stood up at the statue, unable to take my eyes off it. It would be blasphemy somehow to turn away too soon. It captured life, made it eternal. That's what made it so powerful. Michelangelo endowed this solid marble with the life force, created everlasting youth, which most of us think about in one way or another.

We were there for ages, circling it, looking at it from every angle, unwilling to leave it. When we did eventually manage to tear ourselves away, Mrs O giving regretful looks back, we browsed some of the other sculptures but it was all a bit of a comedown after the David.

We walked back out into the stifling heat. We were quiet, unable to find the right words to discuss what we'd just seen.

'It's almost two o'clock,' said Mrs O, looking at her watch. 'Let's find somewhere nice for lunch. We haven't got all that long. They usually close at thrree.'

She seemed to be guided by some kind of personal satnav to a little restaurant called Hosteria Quatro Mori in a quiet, shady side street. We managed to get one of the three tables outside on the tiny terrace.

A waiter appeared bearing a moustache like a villain in a Victorian melodrama, obviously quite a character. Mrs O asked him for a menu and he pointed to his head and said something I couldn't catch.

''E says *'e's* the menu,' explained Mrs O. 'We go' a rright one 'erre.'

On hearing this the Moustache, whose name we learned later was Ricardo, tried out his waiter's English on us, but Mrs O shooed him with her hands and let out a stream of quick-fire Italian. Ricardo gave a little smile and bow.

'They never like giving you the menu,' said Mrs O, lighting up a cigarette.

'Why, do they want to be your guide as to what is fresh and good?'

'They want to pile the food and wine on to you without you noticing, morre like,' said Mrs O, fixing Ricardo with a beady eye.

He was still hovering, brushing off his smart black waistcoat nonchalantly. We weren't sure how much English he understood.

'Let's have a really slap-up lunch,' I said, suddenly in a better mood than I'd been for ages, the lurking sense of panic now almost completely gone. 'On me.'

Mrs O looked delighted and gleefully set about ordering antipasto misto, asparagus risotto and lamb cutlets. She ignored each of Ricardo's further suggestions including the Brunello di Montalcino, dismissing it as too expensive, and asked for a carafe of house red.

'The Brunello's one of the grreatest wines of Italy,' Mrs O told me. 'It's not strrictly Chianti, but it costs a bloody bomb.'

It was a fabulous meal: we were both relaxed, at the same time stimulated by the statue, and the food was very good indeed. The risotto in particular was sensational.

'Would you like some morbid mayonnaise?' asked Mrs O, seeing some on the little cabinet by the entrance. It's one of the jokes between us. I was perplexed when I first saw a jar of *maionese morbido* in the supermarket. I asked Mrs O about what the *morbido* meant. Soft, apparently. As opposed to that hard mayonnaise you see so much of these days. It had tickled her, and we chuckled every time she said it.

At last, when we'd finished eating and leant back in our chairs with sighs of satisfaction and cigarettes, we got to talk about the David.

'It's wonderrful,' said Mrs O. 'Something so vital in something so solid. Wars come an' go bu' therre's always David.'

'Yes, that's how I feel,' I said, downing my glass.

She took a large gulp of hers.

'Y'know, I think we all want rreal life to be like that.'

'Like what?'

'Well, when you find swmmat tha's good, rreally good, you want to prreserve it in stone, keep i' like that' forrever. Bu' you can't. That's wha' the statue does. It keeps swmmat good forrever.'

We took almost two hours over that meal. Ricardo let us take our time as they were closing up.

We strolled back to the car, taking in the sights. It was good being with her. We set off again and this time I even felt relaxed enough to take the motorway down the Arno valley, wordlessly enjoying the view of the hills bathed in the late afternoon sun. Gradually though I noticed something of which I was only vaguely aware on the way up. When I changed into fourth or fifth gear the engine revved up of its own accord for a moment or two. It felt like the clutch was slipping. But I hoped that if I ignored it, it would get better.

When we were nearing Gradoli I asked Mrs O if she wanted to come up for an *aperitivo*.

'Aye, alrrigh' then. I'll joost call in at me sister's to see if she's OK, if you don't mind.'

We stopped off at the block of flats where her sister lived. She was only there for about ten minutes or so. As we drove into the square the crones had already taken up position around their card table outside our front door. These card games were a recent innovation. They'd sit around a foldaway table on camping chairs. Mrs O told me they were playing a game called *Scopa*, which means broom and for which you need special cards. She also said *scopa* was a slang word for fuck.

On the opposite side of the lawn were the – what's a good word for the old men? K had never christened them. Coves? It'll do perhaps, but it's not as good as K's would have been. I can't recapture her. But there's no need. She's still here, all around.

The *Scopa* players gave their slight nods and smiles and *Buona Seras*, but there were the usual disapproving looks as we walked past.

'Do you think they're talking about us?' I asked Mrs O.

'Ohh aye, no doubt.'

'Would they ever say anything to your face?'

'Huh. They better not trry. Orr behind me back for tha' matter.'

'Don't you worry it'll damage your reputation?'

Mrs O cackled.

'I don' think i' cou' get much worse.'

Inside the flat I poured her a glass of her favourite malt and a vodka for myself, and we positioned ourselves on the balcony. I felt an enormous sense of achievement after this first day out in months and something approaching relief. I was almost beginning to enjoy myself. No going back now, I decided. To London. I'd stay put, for good or ill.

I went into the bathroom for a pee and noticed a small trickle of water coming from the inflow pipe by the loo.

'There's a leak in the bathroom now' I announced to Mrs O as I went back in the living room. 'I'll have to get a plumber pretty quick.'

'Come to think of i,' me nephew's son's a plumber. Don' know why I didn't think of 'im before.'

'What, here in Gradoli?'

'Aye.'

'Could you get him here first thing tomorrow?'

'Don' see why not. An' that rreminds me. Therre's someone looking for you.'

'Looking for me?' I asked, feeling a sudden surge of panic. 'Who?'

I must have spoken sharply, because she looked at me in an odd way.

'I dunno,' she says a little indignantly, as if accused of something. 'Some tall, fairr-haired Englishman.'

'Well, what do you know about him?' I asked, trying to sound casual, not too interested. 'What's he asking?'

'Seems 'e was joost in a bar in Bolsena last night, giving out your name. Giulio was there an' popped into see me sister today and he mentioned it. Me sister joost told me about it. That's all I know. Sorry I spoke. Therre's no rreason to get all hoity-toity.'

'Did they tell him anything?'

''Ow should I know?' she said, her voice now rising slightly under this interrogation. 'I told you, I just found out. I shouldn't think the men in the bars know exactly which flat you live in. And as you well know, it's a bi' 'arrd to find at the best of times.'

We both sat alone with our thoughts for a moment or two. Come to think of it, I'd noticed an unfamiliar car in the parking bay under the *piazza* wall the last day or two. Odd, usually the crones are strict about non-residents leaving their cars there.

'Who is it? Who's looking for you?'

'I don't know,' I said, glancing out of the window involuntarily.

But I'd got a pretty good idea.

The Alps and Bolsena, June 10th-12th

I got an early start the next morning and headed further over the Alps towards the Italian border my new destination - Bolsena. It was good to have a project, a purpose I decided. I'm not cut out to be a drifter.

I'd done a quick calculation. It would take me another day or two to get there, and three or four days leisurely drive back to London. That would leave me five or six days to have a good poke around there to find him. A busman's holiday if you like, trying to track someone down, but it gave me a framework for the journey, and that's what I needed.

But after the certainty, doubts crept in as I sped along. I'd thought it would give my trip a purpose, I now began to ask myself what was the point? It seemed a bit of a wild goose chase to go haring round Italy when I didn't know exactly where I was going or why.

I began to go off the idea of going on to Bolsena. I didn't really want to see the Old Git anyway, I told myself. It was just curiosity. What good would come of it? He wouldn't want to see me. No, I'd spend a couple of days here and then start heading back. I'd had enough of freedom and the open road. I found a tiny village just before the border, and asked a farmer if I could pitch my tent for the night. He mimed, 'Welcome.' I offered him some euros but he shook his head and waved them away.

The scenery was stunning. I thought of the *Zen* guy's opinion that you can't see real life through the frame of a car window - you need the wind in your face and your bike on the road. And he says you can't capture the real beauty of panoramic views with a camera - the life is drained out of them. I agree with the first part. but as a photographer, of course, I have to disagree with him about the camera. Think of Ansell Adams - he brought the most barren of landscapes to life. I've only brought my little Sure Shot on this trip, but it's amazing what you can do with the right light and angle etc. I made good use of it.

When the sun began to go down I drove back to the site and wandered into the village. There was one little supermarket and one cafe in the square. I was just going to get what had quickly become my usual supper, but I glanced at the cafe's menu displayed outside. *Steak-frites* were just as cheap as stocking up on basics so I decided to treat myself.

It was an old fashioned little place. It had red and white checked cloths on the small tables near the window, laid for dinner, but the tables further inside just had ashtrays on them.

The bar, like all the cabinets behind it, was cream-painted wood with a tin top. A few locals where leaning on this having their evening drink or two, their heads bent forward in discussion. They turned around and gave me a quick once-over as I went in, then resumed positions.

The barman was listening and nodding and wiping glasses with his apron. I motioned to one of the tables, said, '*Steak-frites*?' with a question mark and he bowed slightly and held out his hand to usher me towards it.

I didn't feel too bad sitting alone at the table for two because a couple of old guys were eating their dinner on the next table, chatting amiably now and again, but they seemed easy with their silences. I felt at home. It must be good to have a mate to mull over the business of the day, especially when you get older. I had an urge to ask them how they became friends, but my French wasn't up to it and anyway it was a daft question. Everyone must know everyone in a place like this. I haven't had a mate like that since the Old Git. I think I've lost the knack of making friends. If I ever had it, that is.

The barman pulled the handle of one of the cupboards behind the bar. It turned out to be a baguette-length bread bin which opened at the top and swung out on its axis at the bottom. For some odd reason this pleased me no end.

He took out a baguette, chopped a few pieces and threw them in a little basket. He brought this over with a carafe of wine covered with a glass. He nodded towards the door and said something. I didn't catch a word so I shrugged and then smiled. He smiled too and set down the bread and wine.

In no time at all he brought over a large plate of steak and chips and little pots of mustard, mayonnaise and ketchup on a tray. It was all delicious, all the more so because of my diet of the last few days.

After I finished and he came to clear away, I pointed at the empty carafe and he brought me another. My two dinner companions of a sort seemed to take this as a signal to bring me into the conversation. Again I shrugged and smiled.

'Eenglish?' asked the one next to me. He was fat, bald, moustachioed and wearing one of those denim jackets.

'*Oui*,' I answered. That was a bit stupid, wasn't it?

His mate pitched in as well. He was slightly younger, thin and dark. Opposites. But I had no better luck understanding him.

The fat one helped out. He made brmbrm noises and twisted his fists forward.

'Yes. I'm on a bike. *Oui*.'

They exchanged knowing looks and laughs, and a couple of the guys at the bar joined in. They seemed interested though. Presently the farmer strolled in and we greeted each other like long lost friends. One of the guys at the bar spoke a bit of English so I managed to convey most of what I wanted to. So we all congregated there and made quite a night of it. They asked some questions about the old bike, what had happened to the British bike and car industry, and then I'm almost sure we moved on to life in the area during the Second World War. I thought of Jo's jokes that my bikes were my friends. Saw myself sitting alone in my garage with my bikes and a whisky of an evening. I could see now what a sad picture it was.

The clientele started making moves about ten and the barman started clearing up. I walked back with the farmer, in companionable silence now that we had lost our translator. We shook hands good night, and I settled down with *Zen* in the tent. I'd ploughed through it - skimming much of it I must admit as a lot was way above my head. That endless quest to define Quality. He wasn't a bit nuts as I thought - he was totally of his fucking head. It made me dizzy just reading about it. Quality just *is,* isn't it? Made up of loads of things. Unlike him and his son, I would say that the time me and the boy had together was quality time, haha. But how would you define it?

I was shocked to read in the Afterword that his son was killed a few years after the trip - stabbed by muggers when he was a student. The guy wrote that even though his body was gone, the pattern he made in the world stayed on. I shed a couple of tears. It made me feel about Dylan's own death in a different way. I made my mind up to press on with the journey to find the Old Git. Life is soon over, and you have to make the most of what you've got.

If I hadn't read the end that night, I might not have finally made up my mind to go. I've been dithering quite a lot, as you well know. Funny how such little random things can affect your life's decisions.

I crossed the border early the next morning. My head was a bit sore but full of a sense of mission again. An urgent mission, because I didn't have all that much time. I had the bit between my teeth.

I stopped at the next garage I came to for some maps. I looked through the racks for Northern Italy but couldn't see Bolsena anywhere. Damn, I thought. Maybe I was wrong after all. I moved down the rack and looked at those for Central Italy. Yes! There it was. I spotted the lake first. The Lago di Bolsena, and the town in the north east corner.

I sat down for a coffee in the little cafe and worked out the route. It was fairly straightforward and it would only take me a few hours from here. I'd be there before evening. The schedule was working out.

I jumped on the bike and sped off down the coastal motorway as far as it went, twisting and turning and tunnelling. After two or three hours it gave way to dual carriageway, and then this alternated with a single carriageway, which was a bit odd given that this seemed to be the main road south. This was no good to man nor beast. As soon as you got a bit of speed up you had to slow down again. It struck me as a dangerous arrangement. The convoys of juggernauts slowed me down quite a bit.

But it was even slower when I left the coastal route and headed for the hills up winding roads, getting stuck behind tiny cars or those three-wheeler trucks that chug along. In these parts at least they seemed to drive either like bats out of hell or at thirty miles a week. You had to be careful round corners. And there were lots and lots and lots of corners.

Eventually I came to a little town called Pitigliano, on an outcrop of rock. I was famished – I looked at my watch and it was about six. I saw a pizza counter outside a cafe where they sold it by the slice. Even better there was a bike park right outside. I walked up to the glass counter – I was a bit stiff and must have been walking like John Wayne – and pointed at the salami pizza and held up four fingers. My Italian's even worse than my French. I ate it on a stone bench with a magnificent view. The pizza was good too – meant to save a slice for later but wolfed the lot.

I must have reached Bolsena at about nine or ten. It was relatively straightforward after all that. It was bigger than I imagined, and quite touristy. I parked the bike on the tree-lined avenue that led down to the lake and had a look around. There were a couple of cafes on the water's edge, one on a kind of pontoon on the lake itself with a gangway leading to it. There were two little marinas either side.

I walked back up the avenue to the main square, hoping to find a cafe where the locals hang out so I could start my enquiries. I found one in a side street, parked myself on a stool at the corner of the bar and had a couple of beers. It looked more German than Italian – sort of Gothic with wooden panelling. There weren't many people in but no-one took any notice of me. I began to think it might not be so easy to track down a Brit round here. They must come and go all the time, on their way between Rome and Tuscany.

Yet again I mulled over exactly what I wanted to accomplish. I still hadn't come up with any firm conclusions. Did I want an apology? To set the record straight? To clear my name, establish my innocence? Or should I, as certain friends had advised at the time, be the bigger man – hold out the olive branch, turn the other cheek? Literally? All this was going round and round in my head when a Brit walked into the bar. He couldn't have been anything else. For a moment I even thought it might be the Old Git himself.

But no. He had greying, wispy, sandy hair which would soon be combed over. Ruddy complexion. A nautical navy and white hooped polo shirt with a red crest. Deck shoes. Not the OG's style at all.

He stood next to me at the bar and nodded. He ordered a beer in confident Italian but even I could tell he had a thick English accent. With the sinking feeling in my stomach that I was going to regret this, I took a deep breath and said, 'Hello.' He reciprocated, and after a couple of mutual sidelong glances we were soon chatting away like acquaintances in the yacht club. Travel and booze can do that.

'Tony,' he said when he thought we'd become friends, and held out his hand.

'David,' I said, shaking it reluctantly.

He soon launched into a long monologue. He and his family were staying at a lakeside campsite south of the town. A nice classy one. All mod cons as they say. This was their third or fourth time here. Drove all the way down. Had a few favourite places such as this. I knew he wasn't my type of guy at all. Full of himself, snobbish, wanting to impress. I had to put up with it. There might be useful information in all that irritating small talk. Eventually he asked what I did.

'I'm a motor mechanic.' I was too tired to go through the celebs routine.

'Oh,' he said. Obviously unimpressed.

At last I managed to get a question of my own in.

'Are there many Brits around here?'

'No, thank God,' he said, laughing heartily and slapping me on the back. 'No, seriously, it's mainly Ities who come up here for the lake. A few Frogs and Swiss on their way back from somewhere. Some German hippy types in old VW vans. But not many Brits.'

'So any Brits who lived here would stick out like a sore thumb?' I decided on the direct approach. He was on his fourth or fifth beer and wouldn't think the question strange.

'Well, I don't know about that. Who are you looking for exactly?'

'Just an old friend.' I gave Griff's name. Was it my imagination, or was there a slight pause in the conversation between the two guys on the table between us and the window.

'Let's ask Luigi here. Hey Luigi!'

'Paolo,' said the barman with a scowl.

'Many Brits live round here?'

'A few, maybe.'

'Where are they stationed?'

'I don't know,' said Paolo. He looked grateful for this ignorance.

'Who would know then?' demanded Tony, as my new found friend insisted I call him in that over-hearty way of his.

But Paolo had lost interest. He shrugged and went up the other end of the bar.

'Sorry mate. Tried me best.'

'Well, it's just someone I knew a long time ago. He's probably long gone now. And I'd better be going myself.'

I couldn't stand much more.

'Oh, yes, you're on your bike, aren't you? Where are you staying? Come down to our site. All the best ones are on the south side.' He said the name, which I instantly forgot. 'We can have a few beers of an evening.'

He clearly considered me quite a pal now.

'Thanks,' I said with a tight smile. 'Might well do.'

'South, remember,' he shouted as I left, pointing upwards.

I got the bike and headed north, back on the road I came in on. I thought I'd find a secluded spot by the lake, and then come back to Bolsena tomorrow to pursue my inquiries.

The road followed the lakeshore on the left for about a mile and then took a swing to the right up the hill. A little side road forked off to the left, following the shore, I imagined. As I swerved to take it a signpost saying Gradoli 3 KM flashed in my headlamp. It was a narrow road with no markings, just wide enough for two cars to pass. After a while it too swung up the hill to the right and I pulled up.

To my left I could see the lake glistening in the starlight through the trunks of pines. There was a gravel lane leading towards it and I took it, the Norton bumping along uncomfortably. It came out in a small cove. There was a kind of snack bar boarded up – just for the winter probably. It didn't look abandoned. There were a few parking spaces next to it, surrounded by the pines. Between them and the lake was a strip of grass and this is where I pitched the tent by the light of the headlamp. I lay down inside and could hear nothing but the hum of insects. Like in old cowboy films, when they're round the camp fire at night. When I was a kid I used to think it was the sound of the projector.

I woke quite late the next morning. All I could hear was the lake lapping and the ducks quacking. For a moment I couldn't think where I was. In France still perhaps, or even by Lake Bala with my family when I was a kid.

It was already hot in the tent. I emerged to find a cloudy sky, for once, and the inviting lake at my feet. I plunged in and yelled out. I expected it to be cold but it was still a shock.

I put all my things besides valuables inside the tent and locked the zip with my little combination padlock. I had no qualms about leaving it. I was sure it would be safe here.

Just as I came to the end of the lane, a car swept round the corner and up the hill, an electric blue Fiat Punto. I hardly had time to look properly but I knew straightaway it was him. The Old Git. I couldn't even tell whether he'd changed much or not. I just sort of recognised his being, if you know what I mean. Sounds a bit daft, but there you are.

Without really thinking I took off after him, my heart pounding a bit as it does on a good chase. As I rounded the corner I just got a glimpse of the one tail light disappearing round the next corner at the top of a fairly long uphill stretch. He was going at a fair lick too.

I opened up the throttle. I was sure to catch him up quickly. When I rounded that next bend, the road became a series of corners. I cut them, taking risks.

They led into the village. Even the main street of the village twisted around in an S-bend, for no good reason that I could see. Otherwise it seemed to consist of this one main street, and a fairly dull one at that. I slowed down and kept an eye out for the car, scanning the few side streets where he might have turned. Nothing.

At the top of the village I opened up again. The road swept up the hill now in a gentle curve as it came to the brow, but it was lined with trees so I could tell how far ahead he was. I must be close on him now.

Then suddenly I hit a T junction with the main road. I had to brake hard and did a little skid. I'd been going too fast. He must have been belting along. To the right a road snaked down a slope back towards Bolsena. Apart from a couple of lorries, it was empty. So I turned left, on a hairpin bend as it climbed up to the top of the ridge. That gave on to a long flat stretch. Two cars were coming towards me in the distance, but there was nothing in front of me.

I turned around, deflated and baffled. He couldn't have got that far ahead. I couldn't see where he could have turned off. I went back down to the village, looking for any lanes or gateways I might have missed on the way up. There were none that I could see where he could have turned off so quickly.

He must have turned off into one of the side streets in the village after all, I decided. But he must have been quick about it. I was sure I was almost on his tail. I went back down to the village and this time I took my time and explored it. It was quite compact. There was the one through road, a handful of side streets, and a warren of narrow, cobbled lanes that didn't look big enough to take even a small car. There were some of those three-wheeler trucks parked here and there.

I went up the side streets one by one. There were a few Fiat Puntos, but none of that kind of blue. Finally I took the little road between the church and the lanes of the old town which ended at some kind of old castle. There was an arch leading into it. It looked as if it gave on to a kind of grass courtyard, surrounded on three sides by the castle and on the fourth a low wall giving sweeping views over the countryside. I edged the bike forward to have a look, without wanting to get into trouble for trespassing. I'm used to being cautious in my job, believe it or not. You have to know the rules.

A couple of women sitting on a bench by a rubbish bin scowled at me. No blue Fiat Punto. I turned around. He must be here somewhere, must live here or have some link with it. Gradoli was clearly the only place the road led to. I'd move my centre of enquiries here, to Gradoli.

Gradoli, June 12th. Morning

There's a buzzing in my ear. I rouse myself from my drowsiness because it might be a wasp or a mosquito. It stops abruptly. My watch says 6.25 am. I concentrate for a moment in the darkness and hear nothing more, so turn over and go back to sleep. It starts again and seems to be coming from the living room. It comes to me that it's the door phone and I experience a shock of panic which jolts me wide awake. I feel certain it's You-Know-Who. Well, you don't know You-Know-Who yet. But I've a feeling you will.

I don't know what to do. I want to ignore it, but realise that this won't get me anywhere in the long term. Something draws me to it. I stumble through the living room, shaking slightly.

When I pick up the door phone I find myself wondering, despite something approaching terror, whether to say '*Pronto*' like they do on the phone, which means 'Ready' and in this case is certainly not the case. Or '*Buongiorno*' as if you were indeed answering the door to someone. It's such an unusual event for someone to ring the bell.

I say '*Si?*'

It's a woman's voice. Something about water coming down the walls. I still don't know what's going on. Do you want me to come down? I ask. It's only then that I work out that the voice is in fact coming from the other side of the front door, not through the phone. It was the doorbell to the flat that rang, not the one to the outside door downstairs. This is an even rarer occurrence.

Feeling foolish, I put the phone down and open the door. Two crones are standing there. Thank God I'm wearing underpants. One is what K used to call the Smiley Crone, who has humour in her eyes and does usually give a quick smile when she says *Buona Sera*. She's not smiling now. She has a habit of thrusting her head back when she's talking to you, as if she's expecting to meet trouble in life and expecting to overcome it.

She indicates her companion, who is not one of the card-playing crones. She lives in the flat underneath, from where mouth-watering smells emanate at mealtimes through the beaded curtain across her open doorway. She's not as alluring as Smiley Crone. In fact she looks a little like a cartoon witch, with missing teeth and a hook nose. Not the fairest in the land. Mind you, she probably thinks the same about me with my tousled hair and saggy pants.

All these thoughts race through my head as I'm bathed in a sense of relief that it's not You-Don't-Know-Who at the door, so I'm not concentrating on what they're saying. They're now looking at me, and when I don't say anything Smiley Crone begins her story again.

There's water coming down the walls of the room below. The witch pitches in and says she woke up and heard this noise. 'Tom, tom, tom' is how she describes it. She speaks quickly and, I suspect, with a slight speech defect or thick accent or both and I don't catch everything she says. It's just as well Smiley Crone feels the need to repeat it.

'Does he speak Italian?' enquires the Witch of Smiley Crone, a little belatedly I feel, as surely we've been having a conversation for the last five minutes.

'Yes, he does,' says Smiley Crone with a solemn nod.

They beckon me downstairs. I point at my pants and then to the bedroom and they nod. I quickly put on some shorts and a T-shirt and follow them down.

We swish through the bead curtains into the kitchen/living-room/dining room where the Witch watches TV of an evening. The set is perched on a high metal trolley as if it's been wheeled in for a presentation. We go through to some kind of windowless parlour, the only light coming through the French windows leading off it into the bedroom. It's packed with tacky ornaments including a lot of coloured glass. A green glass fruit bowl without any fruit in it stands on a plastic lace-effect doily on an octagonal table.

In the corner, by the French windows, I can see a damp trickle running down the wallpaper from the ceiling to a dishcloth on the floor. It's not exactly a cascade but there's clearly a drip coming from somewhere.

'Tom, tom, tom,' the Witch is repeating. I try to work out exactly where the water would be coming from, but it's difficult given that the layouts of the flats are similar but asymmetrical. I look through another door into the triangular room under my kitchen. It's her bathroom, but I think it extends further back than my kitchen, so it could either be coming from the sink or the bathroom.

I rush back upstairs, followed by the crones. I check the kitchen and there's no leak from the u-bend and the tiles beneath the sink are dry. Then with a sudden flash of inspiration I think of the leaking pipe in the bathroom. Of course. Why didn't I think of that before? I dash to the bathroom, but the bowl under the pipe is only half full and the tiles underneath that are dry. So are the ones under the loo, bath, basin and washing machine.

'I can't see any water anywhere,' I say to the crones, who are waiting by the front door. They wait for more.

'Tom, tom, tom,' reprises the Witch.

'What should I do?'

They look at each other, possibly to see which one is actually going to hand over the prize for the most idiotic question of the year.

'Shut off the water,' they say in unison.

'Ah yes. Shut off the water,' I echo. The tap is behind a zinc panel by the outside door. Thank God I know where it is. I run down the stairs, open the panel and turn the red tap. I climb back up and the crones are waiting outside the Witch's flat.

'Has the water stopped?' I ask unhopefully, thinking it could not possibly have acted so quickly.

'*Si*,' they say. '*Va bene.*'

I take a deep breath.

'I can't understand it,' I say. 'There's no water anywhere upstairs.'

'It must be *il tubo,*' says Smiley Crone – the pipe.

'*Si, il tubo,*' I repeat stupidly. 'I'll phone for a…. for a……..,' and cannot think of the word for plumber, but remember it's quite an odd one.

'*Un idraulico,*' supplies Smiley Crone.

'*Ah, si, un idraulico.*'

It sounds like drainage equipment. I go back upstairs and see it's still before seven o'clock. I decide to go back to bed for an hour before ringing Mrs O to see if her nephew can come out. There's nothing to be done right now.

I doze fitfully, half-dreaming of urgent, persistent and terrifying doorbells. When I call Mrs O, she takes a long time to answer and then she sounds sleepy and grumpy.

'We've sprung a leak and the downstairs crone is getting dripped on,' I say.

'Bloody 'ell, you'rre not 'aving much luck wi' water, arre you?'

'Any chance of your nephew coming round now?'

'I'll call 'im and call you back,' she says and puts the phone down.

In fact she doesn't call back but turns up with him about half an hour later. Things can often happen easily and quickly in Italy. The trouble is, there's no knowing when that will be. But think of the hassle and expense you'd have to go through to get a plumber out in London at this time of the morning, and within half an hour. I'm told though that things have got better because of the Poles.

Rossano the nephew is tall and thin and wears a red checked shirt and a pencil behind his ear. He's quiet and businesslike and couldn't be less like his aunt. I take him downstairs and he inspects the Witch's corner in total silence. The Witch follows us and hovers. Rossano doesn't speak to her, or even acknowledge her presence.

I traipse back upstairs behind him. He takes one look in the kitchen and shakes his head. I show him to the bathroom. He looks at the loo and then loses interest, like sniffer dogs in detective programmes. He takes a brief look at the bowl under the leaking pipe, then moves in on the washing machine, instructing me quietly to switch the water back on again.

This time I can only manage a gentle jog down the stairs. This is the most early morning exercise I've had in decades – maybe ever – and I'm already exhausted. By the time I've come back up he's identified the cause of the problem as the inflow pipe of the washing machine, which has come loose by the tap just above it. He's already tightened the tap, and when I wrap my hand round the join I can feel it's still wet but no longer dripping. I hadn't thought of that, but come to think of it, it had to be the washing machine as little else in the bathroom works.

I thank him and ask how much he wants. He waves his hand and shakes his head. I thank him again and start to go downstairs to see if the drips have stopped, but then with a sudden desperation realise that I can't let Rossano go before he takes a look at everything else that's gone wrong. I turn back and find Mrs O sitting in the kitchen drinking her strong black coffee from that tiny cup she likes, smoking a cigarette and reading a book.

'On no account let Rossano go. I think he's fixed the drip and I'm going down to check, but I need him to look at the other stuff.'

Mrs O merely nods wearily. I stagger downstairs again, thinking I'm not long for this world.

'Is it still dry?' I ask the Witch breathlessly.

She's now sitting at her oil-clothed table, drinking coffee and eating a buttered roll.

'*Si, si,*' she says, and seems remarkably calm after the drama.

I explain what happened, and expect her to bring up the subject of compensation for the damage to her wallpaper or whatever, but she doesn't.

'*Va bene?*' I say.

'*Si, va bene.*'

I apologise for all the trouble and she says that these things happen. She's being quite decent about it, I think. I'm not sure I would be placid if the same thing had happened to me at six o'clock in the morning. I think I should offer her something. For some reason I picture the huge preserved leg of ham hanging up in our cool landing, wrapped in a pillowcase to keep the flies of it. This was Mrs O's suggestion. K used to call it the pig in a blanket, and subsequently named it Hamlet. I could offer her Hamlet by way of apology for the trouble caused.

She gladly accepts, so I go up and get it for her and when I plonk Hamlet on her table she looks delighted.

Back in my kitchen, Rossano is now drinking coffee with Mrs O in companionable silence.

' 'E says 'e'll 'ave a look at all the other things wrrong with your waterworks,' says Mrs O.

Rossano looks up and nods silently. I escort him into the bathroom and point out the leak by the loo and the broken siphon, turn on the bath tap that's dried up, and press the shower button which produces no water. He bends over the tap and I leave him to it and go to join Mrs O for a coffee.

In no time at all Rossano creeps back in to join us. He says, using the fewest possible words, that the valve in the tap and the seal on the pipe have gone and he can replace those today - Mrs O helping with the translation. He'll have to order a new shower and siphon. Good, I say, and ask him to get ones like the old ones. He nods and disappears, presumably to get his tools.

Now that this immediate crisis is over, I turn my thoughts to a plan that started forming in my head last night. It seemed a little dramatic, but this morning's events have made my mind up. It wasn't David at the door, but it easily could have been, and I would have been trapped. For by now I'm convinced that the English stranger looking for me is David, the best friend I fell out with several years ago. I can't face him, or the past.

'You'rre quiet,' accuses Mrs O, inspecting me through narrowed eyes.

'I have to go away for two or three days. Something has come up. Can you keep an eye on Rossano and make sure he's OK? Give him some spare keys if he needs to come and go.'

I know it's somewhat ridiculous to run away like this just because an old friend is trying to find me. Until yesterday I'd almost pass out at the thought of leaving the village; now I'm taking off to destinations unknown. But after what happened with David I vowed I'd never see him again and am determined I never will. I've thought about alternatives, and they are even more ridiculous. I can't imagine hiding in my flat with a broken loo, not answering the doorbell for days until I'm sure he's gone.

Mrs O looks dumbfounded to say the least. And there's something else in her eyes. Something I can't read.

'Wherre?' she demands. 'Wherre are you going?'

'I'm not sure,' I answer truthfully. 'But I have to leave now.'

I can tell she thinks I'm holding out on her. She looks at me thoughtfully. She picks up her book from the table and thumbs through it.

'Take this,' she says. 'It's a kind of memoire by Regilda, - you know, the woman who runs the Caffe dei Amici.'

What an odd thing to say at a time like this, I think. She shows me the cover which has a picture taken from the *piazza*, with a view of the hills on the other side of the valley. It's called *Le piccolo cose* - The little things. I thank her, take it, and go into the bedroom and throw a change of clothing and my toilet bag in a holdall along with the book. Rossano returns with his toolbag, and I leave Mrs O in the kitchen.

'Le' me know wherre you are,' she says, staring out of the window as if she doesn't care where I am.

I walk down the steps by the wall in front of the *piazza*. The residents park their cars here in a little bay underneath the wall. It's only when I start up the car that I do seriously begin to consider where I'm going to go. Will two or three days be enough? Surely he's not going to hang around for longer than that?

Oddly enough, I have none of the usual rush of anxiety about leaving the flat, none of the dizziness, the slight feeling of nausea. The source of my anxiety now is around here somewhere, watching, waiting. It's real. I can sense it. I only know that I have to get away. I look around nervously. There's no-one apart from a crone or two waddling back from the shops with wicker baskets. I'm quite desperate now. Nothing will stop me.

I jog down to the little car park below the *piazza* wall and get in the Punto. I rev it up the steep ramp into the square and through the arch, almost hitting the side as I go.

Automatically I set off on the road to Bolsena. But as I get to the lake, I ask myself then what? What would I do there? Rome, rather. Rome is the place to go. You can get lost there, although it's quite small compared to many capitals. Even the thought of the crowds, the tourists, doesn't faze me. Shall I drive or take the train? The train. It'll be easier. No worries about parking. I'll drive over to Montalto and take the train from there. The car will be alright in the little car park for a few days. I'll check into Il Giardino, that little hotel near the Presidential palace, the Quirinale, where you have breakfast on the balcony overlooking the little courtyard with a fountain in the middle. K and I used to stay there on visits to Rome. I can walk there from Termini station. Catch up on a few things

I've always wanted to do. The Palazzo Barberini, for example, that has a good Renaissance collection. It's only about a ten minute walk from the hotel. So I do a quick turn in a lane in a field of maize and head back up in the other direction. I start feeling a little calmer, until I get to the little road going down to the lake. There's a motorbike at the junction, and for one moment I think he hasn't seen me and is going to pull out right in front of me, but he doesn't and I press on.

As I climb the hill, the revving that I noticed on the way back from Florence seems to be getting a lot worse, and it's happening in second and third gear now as well. It'll probably get me to Montalto, I think. But what if it doesn't? What if I break down on the way? My getaway would be foiled. Even as I think this, I can see how ridiculous I'm being.

I pull into a lay-by near the top of the hill and think for a minute, drumming the steering wheel with my fingers. I can't take the risk. The clutch probably just needs adjusting. I'll take it down to my usual garage at the top of town. I could almost freewheel it down from here.

When I get there they're all standing around inside or leaning against the workbenches eating rolls wrapped in foil. Bait, we used to call it on the farm. A mid-morning snack.

'*Buongiorno*,' I say. '*Buongiorno*,' they reply distractedly, and carry on eating. I know better than to interrupt them, so just wait. The one who finishes first wipes his hand on an oily rag as they do and asks me what's wrong.

All the way down the hill I've been trying to think of the word for clutch and it comes to me when I need it. *Frizzione*, like friction.

'*La mia frizzione slitta*,' I say.

'*La friz-zione*,' he corrects my pronunciation. With double letters, you almost have to stop in the middle.

He lifts the bonnet and takes a look, and says almost immediately '*Finito*.' He says it'll take two days to fix and quotes a price which seems a lot for Italy where car repairs are often ridiculously cheap compared to the UK.

'Will it get me to Montalto? I was going to take the train.'

He grimaces and wiggles his hand. He thinks it's not worth the risk. I can see there's nothing else for it, so I get my bag from the car and give him my phone number.

I set off down the street, wondering what next. I could get a taxi to Montalto or Viterbo, but I don't know of any taxi firms here. I see a man drawing up outside the small travel agents and unlock the door. I quicken my step and follow him in.

'Are you open?' I ask.

He gives a shrug as if to say 'Well, you're inside, aren't you?'

He's impatient but not unfriendly. A cigarette pokes out of his shaggy white moustache. He doesn't look as if he's opening up. He's not putting down his briefcase, opening the shutters, looking at his diary on the desk. He looks as if he's just come in to get something.

'Are there any taxi firms in Gradoli?'

'No,' he says, in that definitive Italian way of delivering a one-word negative.

'Car rental?'

'No.'

'Where's the nearest car rental?'

'Viterbo.'

'Would they bring a car over?'

'Ah!' he says, shrugging and raising his hands, which in Italian means, 'Now you're asking!' Indeed I am.

'Pack mule?' I want to enquire, but refrain. Buses are my only hope then. I see them in the town and they must go somewhere. I know the tobacconist opposite the bus stop keeps timetables.

I don't bother to thank the travel agent – just nod politely and turn on my heels. I go into the tobacconist's and ask him for the times of buses to Viterbo. He says the times have just changed and they're never on time anyway. I ask him if he has any idea when the next one is due. He pulls a plastic folder from an old-fashioned wooden drawer and says 11.35 but looks at me as if to say, 'For all the good it'll do you.' Over an hour to wait, maybe more. I feel well and truly trapped, in a way I've never quite felt before. There really does seem no way out. And the enemy is closing in.

I manage to stay calm, and go for a cup of coffee in the Bar Centrale, wondering if this is wise. He might be around here somewhere. I review my options. They are limited. I don't want to go back to the flat. That seems like a retreat. But I can't seem to leave the town either. Is there anywhere I can go?

It's then that I have my brainwave. There's an old monastery on the bigger of the two islands, the Isola Bisentina, which I think is now some kind of hotel, or something between the two. Some kind of sanctuary. I'll go there. Tourist boats go from a little marina this side of Bolsena. They should have started operating for the summer by now. I think they do let you off on the island. I can walk to the marina. It's a good six kilometres but my bag isn't heavy. I can walk part of the way along the lake shore. It's shorter and will keep me off the roads, out of the sight of any passing unwanted old friends.

As I set of down the hill towards the lake, I'm greeted by a whole convoy of gleaming old Cinquecentos, those little Fiats from the Sixties which look like bubble cars. It must be a rally or something, but for a moment I think I'm hallucinating with the stress of it all.

Gradoli, June 12th

After chasing the blue Fiat Punto this morning, I decided to go back down to the lake, relax, and put off thinking about what to do next. I was so near yet so far. I couldn't turn back now. Could I? I bought some salami, cheese, a carton of wine and some water from a tiny shop called Alimentari. It was run by an elderly woman who I think was trying to sell me tomatoes and peaches as well. I just shook my head. Another woman was sitting on a chair by the counter gossiping, like I remember my granny doing in the local grocer's, when we had such things. I had to go to another shop a couple of doors up the narrow street for bread. It was just as tiny, and sold nothing but bread.

I put it all in my rucksack and drove back down to the cove. I stretched out on the grass and, as simple as it was, it tasted good. The wine did its trick and I fell asleep for an hour or so. When I woke up I felt stiff and hot, and the sparkling lake beckoned.

Between the grass and the water was a narrow strip of sand, or gravel more like, and by the water's edge a ring of flotsam – sticks and dead plants mainly. But beyond that the water was clear and the sand below soft. You could see and feel the ridges in the sand. The little waves played the sunlight over the ridges in rhythmic patterns that had an almost hypnotic effect on me, so that I was lulled into some sort of nirvana. The cloud had cleared away completely and everything was very still. The water was inviting.

I plunged in, and swam quite a long way out. Still the bottom wasn't far below my feet. I swam a slow backstroke, looking up at the infinite blue. The silence was broken only by the ducks, the lapping water, or the odd far off drone of a boat motor or a bike roaring up the hill towards the village. It almost seemed as if this moment was what I'd come all this way for.

I swam for a good couple of hours, almost out into the middle of the lake. I got back to the shore knackered and flopped down on a towel in front of my tent. The sun was hot and when I closed my eyes it was as if I was looking into a fire. I felt as if I was slowly disappearing, vanishing into nothing. It was quite a pleasant feeling, the worries of the world far away.

When I woke the fancy suddenly took me to circle the lake. I spread the map out on the grass. The main road didn't make a neat circle around it – it veered off away from it once in a while. But in the places where it did there seemed to be small lanes keeping to the shore. One of them led from the cove and joined the main road just before a place called Capodimonte. On the map it looked like a little peninsula. I looked across to where it should be and thought I could see it – a blob that was darker blue than the rest of the hazy grey hills surrounding the lake.

I set off down the little lane that wiggled round the shore. After a while it petered out to little more than a cart track, and it looked as if it was going to peter out completely. It was a real bone-shaker, and as beautiful as these old machines are, they sometimes make you long for modern comforts.

Soon though the tarmac resumed and I came out on the main road, before turning left for Capodimonte. It was on a rocky promontory with a church or abbey at its apex and a cluster of similar buildings overlooking the lake. I rattled up the cobbled streets to the square, or semi-circle rather, in front of the church and stopped to admire the view over the stone wall. There was a high, sheer drop down to the water below, and quite nearby was the smaller of the two islands, with the bigger one looming up behind it.

On the bigger one, on the only low-lying part by the jetty, was a large building with a bell-tower, half hidden by trees. Some kind of mansion, perhaps. It looked intriguing – inviting somehow.

I had a bite in a cafe and set off again, back to the main road and then up a long, steady climb towards the town of Montefiascone, crowned by a church with a huge gold dome. It seemed like the highest point around the lake, and the view was breathtaking. I could just about make out the pines of my cove on the opposite shore, and above it the jumble of roofs at Gradoli.

Then back down towards Bolsena, past all the camping and caravan sites where my new friend Tony must have been lurking, and I opened up the throttle. At Bolsena I took a left down the avenue to have a daylight look where I came last night. I followed the road around to the marina. It seemed there were boat trips to the islands. There were a handful of people waiting at the end of the jetty. I was tempted. I sat there for quite while deliberating, watching people stroll up and down. In the end I decided I'd done enough for one day. Tomorrow, perhaps.

When I got back to the cove, I found I'd got a text from Jo, saying it was going well in New York, and how and where was I? For some reason I still didn't want to reveal my mission, but stayed as close to the truth as I could and texted back that I was relaxing by an Italian lake.

'Bravo!' she said.

I wondered if it was in fact a mission anymore. I was having such a good time down here by the lake – why spoil it? Idle curiosity, I supposed. I wanted to see how the years had treated him. I didn't have a plan. I thought I'd wander up to the village, find a nice little bar and make some casual enquiries about the Old Git. Pity I hadn't brought a picture of him. I'm not sure I've even got one of him now. Must have all been cleared out over the years. I'd leave the bike here and walk up. It would be a nice evening stroll, and I could have a few drinks without worrying about it.

I set off about a quarter to five. It was a long hot walk, and when I reached the village at about six I was desperate for a beer. I found my way to the Bar Centrale, just this side of the archway I'd peered through this morning. It certainly looked lively enough at first sight. There were a bunch of guys outside, four of them playing cards round a green plastic table and the rest, about three times that number, standing round watching them and shouting – advice, I supposed. They were all quite old.

I went inside and ordered a beer. The barman nodded towards a cold glass cabinet containing bottles of Peroni and Nastro Azzuri. I picked a Peroni and went to sit outside near the card players. There was a whole row of old guys sitting in the green plastic chairs on the pavement, chatting, smoking, reading the paper. There was very little on the tables in front of them: a cup of coffee here, a shot glass of some clear liquid there. It was clearly no drinking den.

I didn't feel like starting to question them straightaway, and I didn't know what to say. So I downed the beer and went inside and got another from the cabinet. I held it up for the barman to see. He was drying coffee cups and nodded. As I went back I could feel myself being observed – not directly, but discreetly, through the corners of eyes. This was obviously not normal behaviour.

After three beers I turned to the old guy next to me, staring blankly at the rest of the village who seemed to be strolling by. I nodded and smiled and said the Old Git's name slowly and clearly, feeling like the stereotypical Brit trying to communicate in a language other than English – a bit like Tony in fact. He obviously thought I was introducing myself, and he shook my hand and resumed his silent staring.

'I'm looking for him,' I persisted, putting my hands up to my eyes like binoculars.

At this my silent companion looked a bit alarmed. I repeated the name, this time with a *Signore* in front.

'Do you know where this man lives?'

Another blank smile.

I took a piece of paper out of my wallet and mimed writing an address on it as if it were an envelope. Even as I was doing it I could see it was ridiculous. He shook my hand again and this time came out with a stream of Italian which sounded like poetry. I didn't understand a word of it.

I looked along the row and went through the same rigmarole with a couple of other old guys. I got the same brief but polite nods and the return to the status quo.

'*Inglesi*,' I said to the row at large, using one of the few Italian words I know, probably from war films or something.

'*Si, si, Inglesi,*' said a couple of the guys wearily, as if to say, 'Yes, you're English. We've got the message.'

Others exchanged remarks in low voices, avoiding my eye. Surely one of them had to know where the Old Git lived. He'd been here for several years now after all.

'Fiat Punto. Blue,' I said, trying another tack.

This time they plain ignored me. I wasn't going to be put off now. The chase was back on. But I was at a bit of a loss. I went in and paid for the beers, and on the way out lingered around the card-players for a moment or two but they were all so engrossed with the game that I figured I wasn't going to get any joy there.

I strolled along to the arch where I'd stopped this morning and sauntered through it as nonchalantly as I could. I saw now that the little road running around the square was a public one, not a private one as I'd thought. There were No Parking signs. Emboldened by the booze, I strode across the lawn. A group of old women were playing cards on a table on the far side, outside a wooden door which was propped open, revealing a marble staircase. I went over to them and said my piece. Only one of them looked up from the cards and said 'No,' shaking her head.

'Fiat Punto Blue. *Inglesi.*'

At that point I could have sworn a couple of them exchanged meaningful glances. One of them said something. I couldn't tell whether it was to me or to one of her friends. I heard, '*Inglesi, no.*' I felt sure there was something going on here, but didn't know what, and didn't know what else to do. I lit a cigarette for something to do and hovered for a while.

The women went on with their game. They shouted at each other as if their lives depended on it. I was leaning on the corner of the main building, where there was a little alleyway between it and another wing. I wasn't looking at them, but I thought I could feel their glances once in a while. The alley had steps leading downwards. Well, not steps exactly, but a sloping cobbled path tiered with a row of little tiles now and again to break the incline. I thought about going down there to explore, but decided against it, as I was still hoping that one of the women might say something. Perhaps they'd talked it over and come up with something.

But no, they were too focussed on their game still. I threw my fag on the ground and toed it out. As I walked back passed them, I thought I heard one of them saying something like '*Francesi.*' That meant French people, didn't it? I swung around and she was pointing up above her. Perhaps she thought I was French. I stood there for moment looking at her but she went back to concentrating on the game.

Oh, well. I'd tried. I walked slowly over to the wall on the third side of the square, my hands in my pockets, trying to look relaxed. I looked over it, and could just about see the lake glinting in the evening sun. I tried to see if I could make out the cove, and thought I recognised the line of trees which bordered it. I walked back through the arch, with one final backward glance at the women. One of them must have won, because there was a thumping of a hand down on the table, and triumphant laughter. I walked back through the arch, and up a little cobbled street, if you could call it that. It was another world, like a film set. There were stairways at angles, and narrow passageways leading off down the hill. In the buildings there were doorways of all shapes and sizes, including some at street level which were little more than barn doors, which I imagined was where the animals were kept when these warrens were built. The grander front doors would be up a few steps. The streets wound up round the big church at the top of the hill.

Somehow I could imagine the OG living here. But if so, where would he put his car? I wandered round, enjoying the views in the golden glow of the setting sun. Still I had the feeling of a failed mission. I'm used to finding my quarry, but here I was foiled by the language barrier. There didn't seem to be anything else I could try. I leant against the parapet of the church square. I could see the square down below and beyond a clearer view of the lake and the cove.

I retraced my steps down to the Bar Centrale, feeling tired and despondent. It was shutting up, the old guys gone. It was barely nine o'clock. There was another bar further up the street. It was called the Caffe di Sport, and was obviously a bit of a hotspot in Gradoli terms. Kids were playing on pinball machines one end and people were watching a football match on TV on the opposite wall. I sank a few more beers there, not even bothering to enquire about the OG. It was not his kind of place, though it was mine. They started closing about ten thirty, so I staggered back down the hill and fell thankfully on top of my sleeping bag inside the tent.

Lago di Bolsena, June 12th. 11.30am

The road to Bolsena was as quiet as the grave after that convoy of Cinquecentos passed. I was nervous, looking around me all the time like a shifty crook. I suppose I was keeping an eye and ear out for any sign of David.

I walked down the hill and round the bend by Condom Cove to the flat stretch of road at the bottom that runs parallel to the lake. In a while I came to a little lane, not much more than a cart track, leading down to the lake through bushes and rushes. I thought it might follow the shore around to the marina, so I took it. It was hot now and eerily quiet, with only the hum of insects and occasional roar of an engine – bike or boat – to break the silence. But at least I was safe here. The track came to an end as it neared the lake, and for a kilometre or two I walked along the gravelly shore. Then I hit a sort of inlet covered in rushes and Spanish Reeds, those tall green plants that thrive around water here. They looked like some kind of mutant corn, and always give me the vague feeling that they are concealing something evil, like that film where malicious children live in a cornfield. *Children of the Corn*, I think it's called.

It grows abundantly in the valley at the back of the *palazzo*. One afternoon not long after K died I went for a walk down the lane that winds along the little river. On the other side there are caves holed out of the tufa rock, many of them with wooden or zinc doors bolted or padlocked, as if they too hold secrets inside. It was hot and still, the silence broken only by the hum of wasps. I almost stepped on a huge dead snake on the road which had obviously been run over mid-slither. As I rounded a bend two large dogs hurled themselves at the rusty wire fence which imprisoned them, barking and snarling madly. This set off a lot of other dogs on nearby plots. I lost my nerve and had to turn back. The whole place had a sinister feel. It reminded me of a local history of the area I read, which said that until the middle of the nineteenth century, it was considered dangerous to go out into the countryside, as it was rife with bandits and malaria. Town gates were shut at night. And malaria only disappeared from the area in the 1950s. It's known as La *Maremma* - The Swamp - and was drained by Mussolini, so I suppose you have to admit that he did do the odd useful thing.

I had the same sense of unease, of menace, now but I couldn't turn back to the safety of my fortress. I skirted the inlet and eventually found myself on the main road north of Bolesena, the Siena road. There was more traffic here and I felt safer. I did try to tell myself not to be so ridiculous, that I was in no danger whatsoever, but I didn't do much good. I felt hunted.

I got to the marina about lunchtime, sweating and breathless, and a little panicky now that something would go wrong with my plan – the tourist boats would not be running, or they would not stop off at the island, or the hotel would not be taking any guests. But on the main jetty was a white signpost saying *Giro Panoramico* with a painted wooden finger pointing towards the other end. There were only a couple of people around, and none near the landing area for the boat trips, but a little wooden clock pointed to quarter to two, which I figured must be the time of the next departure.

I sauntered back along the jetty, watching the ducks coming to sit on the rocks below as if for a breather. At the snack bar the other end I had a couple of slices of pizza and a glass of wine. Back at the landing, half a dozen people were loitering, all Italians. It was gone two now, and way out into the lake, shimmering in the heat, a small boat was chugging its way serenely towards us. The cabin was empty, but two couples were sitting in the open back. A tall young bloke hopped off, moored, helped the couples off, and sold us tickets.

'Does it stop off at the islands?' I asked him when it was my turn.

'One of them,' he said.

'Which one?'

'The bigger one.'

'Is that where the hostel is?'

'We'll tell you all about it on the way. There's a commentary,' he said proudly, and gently pushed me onto the boat.

I took my place at the back, with a young couple who I imagined were on their honeymoon. We headed out into the middle of the lake and the ticket-seller, standing next to the skipper on the little bridge, switched on his microphone with a screech and started his commentary. I reflected that I've never been on the lake in all these years.

'It's the biggest lake in Europe,' he was saying.

That's what Giulio said, so it's obviously an accepted fact in the region. I still found it hard to believe. What about the lakes in northern Italy? K and I had done a tour, staying near Lake Como which seemed at least twice the size of this. One was called *Maggiore* – surely that was a clue?

'I mean the biggest volcanic lake. By circumference,' he added.

Well, how else would you measure a lake, I wondered? Water volume, I supposed. Circumference times average depth. It could be relatively small on the surface, but very deep. Or length. It could be narrow but very long, like Loch Ness. Or if it had a jagged shoreline with lots of inlets and headlands, so that the actual perimeter would be much longer. This lake was mainly smooth along the edge. So lots of lakes could claim to be the biggest in Europe. Why was I moithering about the size of lakes, I wondered? Possibly to distract myself from wondering what the hell I was doing here.

We steered between the islands, and started circling the smaller one: 'the Isola Martana,' screeched the loudspeaker, and then I couldn't catch what he said about it. I strained to hear above the engine, the send of the boat and the screeches. I couldn't tell whether it was inhabited or not. I scanned the wooded slopes for any sign of building, but could see nothing. We were not going to stop anyway – we were going round it.

We started on the second circle of a figure of eight as we rounded the lower end of the larger island. Now I caught more of what he was saying: 'An old monastery.....paying guests.....by arrangement only.....fifteen minutes to look at the magnificent gardens.....not allowed inside the building.'

We moored by the small wooden jetty. I hung back as my fellow travellers clambered up the first flight of steps towards the monastery and darted off to the right behind some cone-shaped box trees towards the gardens. I walked slowly up to the top of the first flight and looked back down towards the jetty. The two boatmen were sitting on the edge, smoking and looking out to the lake.

I took a deep breath and walked boldly up the second flight to the front door, also flanked by conical box in terracotta planters. The wooden outer door was open. I went through the French windows inside and up another couple of steps and stood by the reception desk, behind which a young man was tapping away at a computer. I was relieved to see he was wearing, not a habit, but a suit and tie.

'Name?' he muttered, barely looking up.

'I'm afraid I don't have a reservation.'

'Ah, I'm afraid we only take people with reservations.'

'Don't you have any rooms free at all?'

'Not without a reservation,' he said, now giving me a good look up and down. 'Good day.'

And he went back to his computer. Even in this remote, rarefied place they had to have their computers.

'Isn't this some kind of sanctuary? For people who need to get away and need some shelter?'

He raised his head again and I could tell from the way he tilted it to one side impatiently that he was going to go through his mantra again.

'Look, please help me. I need only a couple of days, but I'm desperate. And I can't get back on the boat now. It's gone.'

In fact I was sure the boat was still there but he was not to know that. He made as if to get up and go out and have a look, but his phone rang so he sat down again to answer it. There was a brief conversation about some administrative detail. I strained to hear if he'd mention an unexpected guest but he didn't. When he'd hung up, he was silent for a moment or two while he weighed me up and then let out a sigh.

'We have certain rules here and like to maintain a spiritual atmosphere and respect the privacy of others. You must hand your mobile phone into reception for the duration of your stay. There are no papers, TV, radio or computers for public use. Meals are simple and at fixed times. I have one small single bedroom. Shared bathroom.'

'Thank you, thank you. I'll take it.'

'For two nights only.'

'That's ideal. Thanks.'

He asked my name but didn't ask to see any identity. Maybe that was part of respecting privacy. So I don't know what made me do it, but I gave a false name. Gareth Williams, which was not all that dissimilar to my own. OK, I didn't want anyone to come here and find me, but how could anyone possibly track me down here? We completed the formalities and I gladly handed over my mobile.

'Is that all you have?' he asked, nodding at my rucksack.

'Yes,' I said.

He looked as if he approved. He handed me an old-fashioned key attached to a large brass disc, and directed me to my room, through an arch to some cloisters then up a wooden staircase to the first floor. This surrounded the cloisters with a polished wooden balustrade, sagging with age. There was something remarkably peaceful about the place.

My room opened off the first floor, which was covered in tiles and mosaics. It was very small, with an iron bed, chair and small desk, a couple of shelves and a wooden coat rack. Perfect. I let out a huge sigh of relief and well-being and put my bag down. I decided against a nap, even though I felt exhausted, and instead took a quick shower in the antiquated bathroom and set about exploring the place.

It was indeed monastic, with barely a soul to be seen. When you did come across someone they seemed to be retreating round a corner, or disappearing behind a closing door, as if they weren't meant to be seen.

The cloisters in particular had a special atmosphere, an almost palpable sense of calm, which was just what I needed at the moment. I walked around them. In the corners were little chapels: no more than gilded altars behind metal grills. Downstairs a corridor opened out of the cloisters. It had stone walls and floor and a couple of small windows. No frills. Out of this opened the refectory, with rows of wooden tables and benches, and next door there was quite a large library, which was a little less stark. It was lined completely by bookcases with fretwork doors. All the books looked very old. There were a few leather armchairs on a silk rug – luxury compared to the rest of the place. No media, as advertised. It all suited me down to the ground.

I took a turn in the gardens, which were terraced down to the lake. They faced towards the south, to the dome of the church at Montefiascone on the hazy horizon, and away from the bustle of Bolsena. I came across a secluded pergola and sat down in the sun, glad to have found my own spot. For the first time in a long, long time I felt happy, alone on my island, and the shimmering of the lake in the late afternoon sun set me dozing. As I closed my eyes, there was a blaze of red, orange and pink light. The sun was hot on my face like fire, but the breeze from the lake gave little icy tickles. It was as if I was being transported out of time.

When I came to, there was an old man sitting on the next bench along. I can safely say old, because his face was lined with what I can only describe as Biblical wrinkles. Like Methusala. But etched into each one of those wrinkles were wisdom and kindness, and they bunched up around startlingly vital and smiling eyes.

We exchanged polite smiles. But, trying to keep in with the unspoken rules of the place, I got up to go. Supper would be soon.

I gave him a smiling nod goodbye, but as I did so he raised a quizzical eyebrow then patted the bench next to him in a commanding invitation. Somewhat robotically, I obeyed. I stole a glance at him from the corner of my eye. He didn't belong to the monastery,

I would say. Tall and lean with a shock of white hair and old-fashioned black round glasses. A retired teacher, possibly, or a writer. Roman, probably. And despite those piercing eyes, his body seemed to be withering away - his skin was so pale that there didn't seem enough blood to go around his body. Was he also seeking sanctuary? If so, from what?

'It's so beautiful here, isn't it? It restores the soul.'

'Yes, so beautiful.'

He was silent a moment or two. I couldn't tell whether he was lost in thought or waiting to say something more. I was conscious that I shouldn't intrude on his privacy, and presumably he was thinking the same about mine, so it made conversation somewhat of a challenge. Yet I couldn't help feeling he wanted to get something of his chest. Or was he waiting for me to say something, or ask something? But it was he who made the first move.

'Peaceful,' he said, taking in a deep breath.

'Yes,' I had to agree. 'But I suppose it could get very lonely after a while.'

That faraway look came over him again.

'Lonely is my lot,' he said, 'I have no-one now. But it's not a bad place to be alone. I feel at peace.'

We both followed a tourist boat skirting the island.

'It's where my journey will end,' he said. And then he turned to me. 'But you're still on your way.'

He said it kindly, as a simple statement of fact.

'On my way where?'

'Oh, I can't say. Even you can't say. Not yet, anyway.'

He spoke in an old-fashioned way. He used the formal *lei* address to me.

'You're not from here, are you?'

'No.'

'Your Italian is very good. Polished.'

'Thanks. I've lived here a long time.'

'And you came from....?'

'Wales.'

'Ah, Wales.' He seemed delighted. 'Hills and mists and castles.'

'Yes, we have those. Have you been there?'

He seemed to go back into the mists of time.

'Long ago.'

'You've been to lots of places?'

'Yes. And now I'm here.'

'Well, as you say, not a bad place to end up.'

'Indeed not. But it is the saddest thing in the world to be alone. Wouldn't you agree?'

'Some people need to be alone.'

'Need, no. Choose, yes. For whatever reason. You don't need to be. I perforce have to be. There's a difference. There's a difference between being alone and being lonely. Which are you?'

I couldn't take my eyes off those wrinkles of wisdom. Yet I was beginning to resent his sermon, find it ridiculous even.

'I've got to like being alone,' I said. 'I used to know lots of people.'

'That can be just as bad as knowing nobody,' said this odd old sage.

I thought about this for a moment.

'We all need people we can go to when we're in trouble,' he said. 'And people need us, too. Never forget that. We're all here for a reason.'

'Here on earth, or here on the island?'

'Both,' he said.

'Well, it's time for dinner,' I said. 'Would you like to come with me?'

'So kind. Very nice of you to ask. But I think I'll stay here a while.' Still that formal *lei*. He. He spoke of me in the third person. As if I wasn't there. 'Very nice of him to ask.' I'd have expected him to switch to *voi* by now.

'Well, if you're sure,' I said, losing patience with his eccentric, studied ways. 'Aren't you getting chilly?'

'A little. But I'll enjoy the last of the sun while I can. It's been a good day. And I've made a delightful new friend. Your name, if I may ask?'

'Griff,' I said, and straightaway realised I was here under an alias.

'Delighted, Griff,' he said, half rising from his seat and extending his hand which I shook. 'Massimo.'

'Nice meeting you too, Massimo.'

'And Griff,' he called as I walked away.

'Yes?'

'Don't make solitude your friend before you have to. Your life is basically a conversation in your head. You can change it any time you want.'

Supper was in the refectory at half past seven. It would give me the first opportunity to get a good look at the other fellow guests. They seemed mainly to be on their own, although there was one elderly couple, all Italian. I tried to discern if they had anything else in common, but they were a variety of ages and, I would say, backgrounds. We exchanged greetings politely, but there wasn't much chatter. Clearly people were here for a contemplative life. Massimo must be quite an exception. I wondered what they were seeking sanctuary from, how they had found the place, and how long they were staying. Maybe they had been referred here by their priest or doctor. I kept a reluctant eye out for Massimo, and was relieved when he didn't appear.

The food was simple and good: prosciutto, pasta, salad, cheese and fruit, with carafes of water and wine. Afterwards I went for a stroll outside, for some reason avoiding the bench overlooking the headland where I'd met Massimo. And then came the question of how to spend the rest of the evening. No phone, no buxom temptresses in an old film. I thought of Regilda's book in my bag, went up to get it and took it into the library. It wasn't very long and I soon finished it. It turned out she used to live in *La Rocca* as a child. She wrote about the hardships after the war – the scarcity of food, the cold winters, the lack of heating, just as Mrs O described. Her father used to warm her bed with his own body. At the end was a poem: *Piccolo Pensiero* – Little Thought.

L'amore non sempre arriva
Da strade primarie

Puo arrivare da stradine secondary
Sconesse con mezzi di fortuna
Arriva piano piano al vostro cuore
Se rimarrete in silenzio
Lo riconoscerete e inconfondibile
Non potete sbagliare
Puo avere occhi azzurri o neri
Puo essere biondo o bruno
Alto o basso
Bello o bruto
Lo riconoscerete dalla sua tenerezza
Dalla sua passione
Dal suo rispetto
Quando avvertite che per quell'amore
Voi siete tutto, l'universo
Il caldo sole, la romanitca luna
Un mare di passion, un gioiello prezioso
Fategli spazio nel vostro cuore
Accoglietelo con amore e lealta
Donategli tutto di voi
Senza riserve.

Love doesn't always come
Along main roads
It can come along byroads
It wanders around with good luck to give out
It goes gently gently into your heart

If you stay quiet
You'll recognise it, it's unmistakable
You can't get it wrong
It can have blue or black eyes
It can be fair or dark
Tall or short
Pretty or plain
You'll recognise it from its tenderness
From its passion
From its respect
When you feel that with this love
You are everything, the whole world
The hot sun, the romantic moon
An ocean of passion, a precious jewel
Make space for it in your heart
Welcome it with love and loyalty
Give it all your being
Without reservation.

I was ready for bed by half past ten, long before my usual hour. As I settled down for the night, I thought about Regilda's poem, and Massimo's words. They were comforting, somehow. Perhaps I had indeed forgotten what it was like to be needed. Perhaps I had been a fool, shutting myself away from the world. And now this whole mad melodrama I'd embarked on to hide from an old friend struck me as preposterous. Maybe it was time to face the truth.

I slept the sleep of the dead, and woke this morning refreshed and clear-headed. I got up early and poked my head through the refectory door. There was no one about, although some clanking sounds were coming from what I took to be the kitchen beyond. I walked down to the lake to wait for breakfast. There wasn't a soul about. Yesterday's sense of peace was still with me. A motor launch that I didn't see yesterday was bobbing about by the jetty. I'm not exactly sure what a motor launch is but I'm pretty certain this was one – all polished wood and chrome. Pale blue and white striped upholstery.

By the time I went back up to the refectory a simple breakfast of bread and jams and jugs of coffee had been laid out on the sideboard. People sauntered in in dribs and drabs, repeating last night's ritual of polite nods and civilised silence. I examined them again, as discretely as I could, wondering what their stories were, whether there was a common denominator. But only their ordinariness seemed to connect them. Maybe they were running away from something like me, or simply seeking a bit of peace and quiet. Or were they, as Massimo had seemed to suggest, in search of something they didn't know they'd lost. But someone said if you're running away from something, it means you're running towards something too. I found myself suddenly infuriated by his enigmas, his guessing games. My daughter used to have a postcard on her bedroom wall saying 'Keep it simple' and next to it 'Stop the world, I want to get off.' Maybe they just wanted to get off the world for a while.

I couldn't make out the place either. Was it all as simple as appeared on the surface, or was there something behind it all? When locals talked about it, they'd use phrases like 'a sort of monastery,' or 'some kind of retreat.' Were people sent here?

I lingered over breakfast until they'd cleared away. I began to wonder how I would spend the day. I have to confess that I was already missing the news. How quickly can a sense of peace begin to get a bit boring. I'd brought the book I was reading on the Medicis, but it was a bit heavy going. The ones in the library were largely ecclesiastical or spiritual, and I didn't fancy that. I'd already given the garden a thorough going over. I could explore the rest of the island, I supposed. Most of it looked steep and rocky, even a little menacing, but I was sure there were places you could walk. I'd ask at reception.

It was the same man as yesterday. Before I asked him about the walks, I thought I'd better let Mrs O know here I was. I'd left in a bit of a hurry yesterday, and was beginning to feel guilty. Maybe she'd know a bit more about the place too.

'*Buongiorno,*' he said as I approached, bowing his head slightly.

'*Buongiorno,*' I replied. 'Could I have my mobile phone back for just a moment please?'

'I'm sorry, sir. I made it quite clear when you booked in that mobile phones are returned only when you leave. We have strict rules and you agreed to bide by them.'

'Yes, but I have to make just one phone call to let someone know that I'm OK. I left in a bit of a rush yesterday.'

He shot me a look from the top of his eyes that was full of meaning, and that meaning was 'I knew as soon as I laid eyes on you that you'd be trouble.'

I countered by staring pointedly at the phone on his desk.

'Very well,' he sighed, 'if it's very important you can make one phone call from here. But that'll be your last.' That sounded ominous.

I didn't particularly want to make the call right there in front of him but was aware that I was in no position to ask for privacy. I rang Mrs O's mobile.

'*Pronto,*' said the husky, impatient voice.

'Ah, morning Mrs O. It's me.'

'Oh, aye? And wherre's me exactly?'

'Not far away. I just needed to get away for a couple of days.'

'Well, you can just get yourrself back here strraight away. Your niece has been looking for you.'

I think I must have let out a little gasp. 'My niece? In the flat?'

'She was, yesterday afternoon. She's on her way from Florence to Rrome or somewherre. I didn't know where you werre, or when you'd be back. And I couldn't get hold of you on the phone.'

'Where's she gone now?' This was dreadful news.

'I think she was going to stay in Bolsena last night, and has to leave this evening. She was going to come back this morning to see if you'rre herre. So you'd better get back, pronto.'

She put the phone down, and so did I. I think I must have leant on the desk for a moment or two, for support. My knees and hands were trembling slightly. My niece. And David. In the same place at the same time. Good God! This is how the whole trouble started in the first place. What if they were to meet? No, I must prevent that at all costs. I must have sunk a little lower, clutching the desk with white knuckles.

'*Va bene, signore?*' asked the receptionist, raising a quizzical eyebrow in the most ruffled state I'd so far seen him.

'*Prego? No, va male. Va molto male.*'

Gradoli, June 13th. 8am

I woke slowly the next morning, hungover and dehydrated. I swigged warm water from the bottle in my tent. I spat most of it out. I'd forgotten to leave it in the lake, tied on a string to keep it cool as I usually did. It didn't do much to quench my thirst. I went outside and had a pee, and refilled the bottle with the cold lake water. There were clouds hugging the tops of the hills surrounding the lake, but it was already getting warm. Knowing it was a mistake, I lay back down in the tent with the flaps open and went back to sleep.

I came to an hour or so later feeling even groggier, so I ran out and plunged in the lake. The shock of the cold woke me up in an instant. I kept swimming, hugging the shoreline towards the town, until I hit a patch of reeds just beyond the little headland at the end of the cove. I turned back and staggered out of the water, refreshed. I towelled myself off a bit and sat on the grass in the pale early morning sun. In some ways I felt I'd done what I could to find the OG. I only had a week or so of leave left. I could see a bit more of Italy – Rome perhaps – before heading back.

On the other hand, I was pretty sure the OG must live in that old *palazzo* through the arch somewhere, and it irked me to be so close and so far. The mystery was, where he kept the blue Fiat Punto.

I formulated yet another plan. I'd pack up and leave today, but have one more look for it before I went. I'd buy an envelope and write his name on it – maybe the people last night hadn't understood the name the way I said it. That way I could pretend I was delivering something. I wouldn't look so suspicious just hanging around, and people might be more inclined to help me out. Then I could leave him a note if I did find where he lived but he was out. Leave him my mobile number. Call in on the way back from Rome, if he was willing. Because I think now I did want to have it out with him, get some closure on this thing that had come between us.

I pulled down the tent and packed up quickly. When I got to the village I parked the bike in the little square where the post office was. I managed to find a notepad and an envelope in the tobacconist's. I strolled up one of the narrow little streets and found a nice place called the Caffe degli Amici. I ordered a coffee and sat down outside to compose the note. This is what I came up with.

Griff: I was in the area and tried to look you up. No luck, obviously. Just wanted to see how you were, after all these years. Get in touch if you feel like it. I might head down to Rome and could call in on the way back in a day or so. David.

I thought it better not to mention anything about fights, or rifts, or accusations. I left my address. He must have it. And my mobile and email, which he couldn't have. It's been that long since we saw each other. Perhaps it's easier to send a text or email, than write or make a call.

I suppose I did want to know how he was. I don't really bear him any ill will. Never did. No matter how badly he behaved. And now the anger has largely subsided.

I put the note in the envelope, wrote his name, and put it in my pocket. I walked back to the bike, started it up, and drove towards the arch. Then everything went black.

Isola Bisentina, June 13th. 9am

In a way I was lucky that I did make that call by the desk, with the receptionist there. He must have gathered there was some kind of emergency.

'I need to get back to the mainland immediately,' I said a little shakily, my chest tightening.

He threw up his hand a little in that familiar gesture which says, 'What do you expect me to do about it?'

'The next boat isn't due for another two hours,' he said, looking at his watch.

'I can't wait two hours. I must get back to Bolsena as soon as possible. It's extremely important.'

I stopped short of saying it was a matter of life and death, because it sounded too fake, or melodramatic. But that's what it felt like. The irony was I didn't particularly want to go back to face the music, but I knew I had to. It was as if I were driven. There was no hesitation whatsoever.

The receptionist was just looking at me in a long-suffering kind of way.

'What about that boat down there?' I demanded, flinging my arm behind me towards the front door.

'What boat?'

I didn't know the Italian for motor launch. 'That boat down by the jetty.'

'*Signore*,' he sighed, 'I've told you we do things only by advance booking. I let you have the room in the first place because you were here and seemed so desperate to stay. But........'

I decided to tell it him like it was.

'And I'm very, very grateful. But I have to go now. My niece is waiting for me, and she only has a few hours. I haven't seen her for years and there's something terribly important we have to sort out. I'll gladly pay for both nights.'

The family card is always a bit of a trump in Italy. He thought about it for a moment or two.

'I'll see if anyone's free to take you, *Signore,*' he said, picking up the phone, 'and of course you will pay only for the night you stayed here.'

It all happened quickly after that. He said someone would be able to take me to Bolsena in ten minutes, but it would have to be ten minutes and not a minute longer. I hurried up to my room without actually breaking into a run, out of respect for the place, stuffed my things into the bag, came back down and handed him over the cash for the night. He handed me back my phone and said '*Buona fortuna, Signore*' with a little smile.

Somewhat buoyed by this, I bounded down the steps as fast as decorum would allow, and sure enough, a weather-beaten old man with a grey beard was waiting in a purring launch I hadn't seen before. I jumped in and as we roared off I looked back at the mysterious place with a tinge of regret.

As we left the jetty, another boat passed us by in a somewhat stately fashion. It was an odd boat, low, with one long window running its length. On the top of that low window, on the inside, were ruched curtains. They were black. It was a hearse boat. And in an instant I knew it had come for Massimo.

And now I think I have to say what this is all about. I wasn't going to of course. I've never told anyone the whole story, not even K, although I think she must have worked out most of it and guessed the rest. But now I see I must write it down here or write no more.

It was in the late nineties, when we were still living in London. My niece Lily was then a struggling actress, getting bit parts in this and that, and living with a rather well-known actor. I won't name him, but you may be able to guess. It was one of the hottest stories in the tabloids at the time. Then he ran off with one of the co-stars of his latest film, who was reportedly supplying him with drugs (this turned out not to be true).

Lily was devastated and went to stay with her brother Nat, partly for a shoulder to cry on, and partly to avoid the press who'd camped outside her flat. They wanted her story and pictures of her breaking down, but were also desperate to find her boyfriend, or ex as I suppose he was by then, who'd also gone into hiding. They thought she might spill the beans through spite. Of course she wouldn't have.

David was my best friend, and a photographer. I'd known him for years. He was one of K's old Fleet Street crowd, and he and Jo lived near us in Clapham. We were in and out of each other's houses all the time. David and I were very close. We had one of those relationships that some women think men don't have: we used to confide in each other, discuss each other's problems, ask each other for advice. All over a few drinks, to be sure.

I was always very proud to have him as a friend. He was so different from the somewhat effete bunch in publishing. He was a very strong character, not very confident in groups of people, but he was his own man. Unlike me, he was sporty, handy. He could turn his hand to anything: strip an engine, tile a floor, build a garage. Apart from anything else, he was very useful to have around. And when we were younger I loved whizzing around London on the back of his bike.

Yet for all our years of closeness, there was sometimes a distance. It was as if we were jealous of each other, weren't confident enough of the friendship to enjoy it simply. We'd have arguments and then sulk for a few days. In some ways we were like two teenagers. We should have trusted each other more.

In those days David was doing freelance shifts on one of the top tabloids, and wanted a job there. Tracking either Lily or her ex down would secure this, in his view. He came round one Saturday morning, as he often did before he started his shift. K was out, so there was only me there. Lily had phoned me earlier, distraught. Her parents had already emigrated to Australia, so she only had her brother and us for family. She'd rung to tell me she was moving in with Nat. She said she was going to lay low there for a while until all the ballyhoo died down. I wasn't sure I had Nat's address so I asked for it. I'd just written it down in my filofax – we all had them then - when the doorbell rang. It was David. I ushered him into the living room and went to make the coffee. He got round to talking about Lily. He was on his way to her old flat. I accepted that this was part of his job and didn't try to stand in his way. He asked me I knew where she was and I said I wouldn't tell him if I did. He nodded, accepting that. We chatted for a while and he left.

It was only later when I was tidying up a bit and went to take my filofax from the desk in the living room that I noticed there was a blank page where Nat's contact details should have been. This was before most people had mobile phones. David was the first person I knew to have one; it was the size of a brick. I'd only just got mine. So it was important to have people's addresses.

I remembered I'd had to start a new page for it, so only his address would have been on it. I flicked back and fore, trying to find it somewhere else but with no success. David knew Lily and Nat and he would put two and two together. But I wanted to give him the benefit of the doubt. Maybe I hadn't written it down after all, I reasoned, even though I could distinctly recall picking up the pen and doing it. It niggled me for the rest of the day.

When I went to get the Sunday papers the next morning, Lily's teary face was splashed all over the front page of the tabloid, with David's picture by-line underneath. It was taken on the street in Islington where Nat lived. Lily was trying to hide her face but you could see the anguish on it. It was a good picture.

I was outraged. He must have taken that filofax page - there was no other explanation. But I still couldn't quite believe it. In all the years I'd known him, I'd always thought of him as an honourable man. Trying to track her down was one thing, but stealing a page out of my filofax quite another.

When I got back I flung the paper down on the kitchen table where K was drinking coffee.

'Oh dear,' she said quietly.

'Oh dear indeed,' I said, rather more loudly.

'What are you going to do about it?' she asked, after a pause.

I didn't know. I didn't tell her about the missing page. I never did. The phone rang. It was Lily, sobbing so hard I could barely make out what she was saying. Gradually she calmed down a little. I thought she'd come out and ask me if I'd given David the address but she didn't. She didn't mention him at all in fact. I wondered if she'd forgotten I'd asked for it, or didn't recognise David's surname. Maybe she was waiting for me to say something, but I didn't because I had no proof. I sensed something unspoken between us though: a silent suspicion on her part, a guilty guile on mine. I asked her round to lunch but she didn't want to leave the flat. There was a pack of them outside, she said.

My relationship with Lily suffered. We'd always been quite close but now we drifted apart, without acknowledging it. The actor's career took a nosedive, and in time the media lost interest in him and Lily, but things were never quite the same again.

As for David, I didn't see him for several days. Neither of us made contact until the Friday, when we usually met for a drink. He texted me.

>Windmill?

It was like a summons, despite the question mark. He was a very economical texter. The Windmill on Clapham Common was one of our locals. I hoped he was going to come clean, and apologise, so I accepted the invitation.

'How was your week?' he asked as we sat down with our pints.

'OK. Yours?'

'Not bad.'

We were circling around each other. After he came back from the bar with the next round, I said, 'I saw your pic.'

'Which one?'

'You know full well which one. She was distraught'

'Well, I'm sorry about that. Truly. It's my job.'

'How'd you get her address?'

'You know I can't reveal my sources,' he said with a wry smile.

'Not even if it was me?'

'What?'

'The address was in my open filofax when you came round last Saturday morning.'

'So what are you saying exactly?'

'I'm not saying, I'm asking.'

'Asking what?'

'Alright, I'll spell it out for you. Did you or did you not take the address from my filofax?'

'So you're accusing me now?'

'I just want an answer.'

'After all these years, you think I'd do something like that?'

But he wouldn't deny it. I asked him point blank, but he refused. Then he picked up his pint, threw it over me, and stormed out. I sat there for a while, too embarrassed to move. When I'd stopped dripping, I got up and went out too. He was standing outside, smoking. He went to say something. I hit him. It was a kind of reflex action. I'm not making excuses or trying to justify it. I'm not proud of it. Something snapped and I hit him. Not a punch, but a slap on the side of the head. Quite a hard one. Neither of us said anything. I turned and walked home. Fortunately K was out to so I'd showered and changed by the time she came home.

I'd calmed down a little the next day and sent him a text asking how he was. As I expected, there was no reply. There never was. We haven't spoken from that day to this. Best friends must differ, my dad used to say. We were different. And differ we did. And differ we do.

Writing all this down now, it doesn't seem like such a big deal. It must have been festering deep down for all these years. Thinking about it, I don't even know what I was most angry about - his theft, his denial, or the thrown pint. Massimo's words came back to me: it's a choice.

It's two or three years since I've seen Lily, too. Fair enough, she travels a lot now. Her career's taken her all over the world. And now it's brought her to Bolsena. Naturally, I'm nervous of seeing her again. Especially with David lurking around somewhere. In a way it's what I've been dreading, all these years, something like this happening. And in a very weird kind of way as well, it's a relief.

I mull all this over in the boat. When we land I almost run up the avenue leading up to the town centre, try to remember if I've ever seen any taxis here. I think I have, but have no idea where the rank or office would be.

It's now about eleven. I ring Mrs O to see if Lily has left her number. If she's in Bolsena, maybe we could meet up here. But she hasn't.

'She just said she'd come back later on this morning,' says Mrs O. 'Wherre are you now?'

'Bolsena. Back as soon as I can. Keep her there if she comes. Bye.'

On one of those very rare occasions when you feel things are going your way, when I get to the central square I see a blue bus with a Valentano sign on the front waiting by the traffic lights. That's the town at the top of the hill above Gradoli. It must stop there. I remember there's a Post Office just to the left of this square, and there are usually bus stops at Post Offices. I run around the corner, and lo and behold there is a stop there. The bus squeals to a halt, and the doors hiss open.

'Gradoli?' I pant, and the driver nods. I flop gratefully down into the nearest seat.

When I get back to the flat it's coming up to lunchtime. Lily has not yet put in an appearance, and time is getting on. Mrs O, I can tell, realises I'm in a bit of a state. She's unusually attentive.

'You sit down and I'll mek you swmmat to eat,'

'I'm not hungry,' I say like a sulky teenager.

'Well, you need swmmat inside you. Then I'll brring you up to date with everything.'

She must have prepared something already, as she quickly serves up *bruschetta* followed by a bowl of spaghetti and meatballs, which she knows is my favourite. I ask her if she is having some but she says she'll have something later with her sister. Once I start eating, I feel suddenly ravenous. I do feel better.

'At least Rossano has mended the loo and the bath,' she says. ''E's orrderring a shower and that other thing. So 'e should be back next week.'

This is indeed something. One less thing to worry about.

'Thanks for that,' I say. She shrugs it off. 'Now tell me about Lily,'

'Well, it werre about half an hour after you left. The doorbell goes, and as you know it don't go that often. I fair joomped out o' me skin. Especially wi' Rossano banging about in there. So I pick up the phone and say swmmat in Italian. Can't rremember what. And then this quite rrefined voice asks in English if it's the rright addrress for you. So I say aye, and then she says she's your niece an' all, so I say you're not herre at present, but does she want to come up, and she says aye arright, or rrather "Ooh yes, I don't mind if I do."'

Mrs O affects a somewhat pantomime version of a posh accent which doesn't quite come off.

'So she comes up and I mek her a coop o' coffee. I explain you've gone away for a day or two, but I'll trry to get hold of you. She says she's been in Florence and is driving to Rrome. She hasn't got mooch time but she'll call back herre late this morning.'

She looks at her watch.

'I wonder wherre she is.'

'Did she say if she wanted anything in particular?'

'Nooooo,' reflects Mrs O, 'she just says she werre passing and decided to come and look you up. A niece can look up herr uncle, can't she?'

'How did she look?'

'Oh verry nice, verry elegant', says Mrs O, smoothing down her sides and doing a little wiggle.

'Well? Happy?'

'Oh, aye. Why are you so worried about seeing her?'

'Oh well, I haven't seen her for a long time, that's all. We sort of drifted apart.'

There's a slight pause.

'Therre's something else,' says Mrs O rather cagily, lighting up a cigarette.

'What?' I ask, almost spluttering on my wine.

'That frriend of yours, or that man who came looking forr you, 'e 'ad an accident yesterrday morrning.'

'Accident? Where?' I feel panic welling up again.

'Just inside the archway. 'E werre knocked over'.

'How is he?'

'Not too good, apparently. 'E werre taken to Viterbo. In a coma.'

'How do you know all this?'

Even the Gradoli grapevine wasn't this good.

'The police came herre yesterday, and again this morning'

'The police?' I screech. 'What the hell do they want?'

''E werre carrying an envelope wi' your name on it. I tell you, I've 'ad one 'ell of a morning of it, wha' wi' one thing or another. They want to see you.'

'Who?'

'The cops. Rroutine enquiries, they said, or whatever they do say.'

The doorbell makes us both jump. We look at each other, as if we have to decide what to do. I get up from the table with a scrape of the chair and go into the living room and pick up the speakerphone nervously.

'Hello?' I say in English.

It's Lily. She sounds exactly as I remember her and is cheerful, as if nothing ever came between us. When she comes up she looks radiant and, as Mrs O said, elegant, wearing a cream linen suit with a wine-coloured silk scarf round her neck. She hugs me and kisses me on both cheeks.

'How fab to see you, Uncky,' she says.

'You've already met Mrs O,' I say, for lack of something better.

They nod and smile at each other, and Lily gives a little wave and says 'Hi again' Mrs O offers her some lunch but Lily says she's already eaten so Mrs O bustles into the kitchen to make coffee.

We go out onto the little balcony and sit at the table. It's extraordinarily good to see her. She's far more at ease than I am, and chats away merrily like she used to. Her present project is a film about Lucrezia Borgia, which portrays her, not as the scheming incestuous poisoner that history has painted, but a pawn in the hands of her father and brothers who use her for their own political ends. Not the lead role, but a good one. They've been shooting in Florence and she's now on her way to Spoleto, where Lucrezia was installed by her father as governor at the age of nineteen, and then on to Cinecitta in Rome. She looked Gradoli up on the map and found it was about half way, so she hired a car in Florence and drove.

She apologises for not being in touch for so long. She'd been busy, buzzing here and there, living out of suitcases.

'You know what it's like when you're starting out and working really hard at something you want to do,' she says. 'It's all you have time for. It's only when you have some success that you start to remember there are other important things in your life.'

She's looking at me earnestly, steadily. Maybe I've been wrong about the unspoken gulf between us, then. Maybe there hasn't been any. She doesn't even seem to have any suspicions about my role in her media ordeal. I wonder whether to bring it up.

'I'm just happy you're here,' I say.

I can hear Mrs O clanking crockery and cutlery in the kitchen. 'I thought for a while after that whole press thingy that......well, that you blamed me in some way.'

'Oh? For what?'

She seems genuinely curious.

'Well, you know, I had friends in the tabloids. You might have thought one of them.....'

'Oh, I know who let the cat out of the bag about where I was,' says Lily with a shake of her head. 'It was my old flatmate. She was going out with a hack at the time. She didn't mean anything by it. She just wasn't thinking. She came round to apologize later, but I wasn't even that angry after the whole media circus moved on. She soon dumped the sleazebag. But all that's water under the bridge. Fancy you worrying about a thing like that. Unlike you, Unc.'

I feel dizzy and queasy. Mrs O brings out the coffee, and I gulp some down as soon as she pours it, burning my mouth. It's true. I didn't used to worry about things, but lately it seems I can't stop. What Lily has just said is astounding. It means I've been wrong all these years, and I was wrong to accuse David in the first place.

No – wait! It doesn't necessarily mean that he didn't take the filo-fax page. It just means that the tabloids were tipped off by another source as well. But still, it does turn my world upside down a little. A world in which I had grown disillusioned with friendships, relationships, had thought myself bereft of love after K died. Alone.

Lily is saying something to me.

'How is he now?'

'Who?'

'Your friend. David. The photographer.'

'Well, I haven't seen him for some time..........,' I stutter and notice Mrs O giving me a meaningful look under raised eyebrows. She's probably worked a lot of it out too by now.

'......but in fact he's, well, I think he may have come here the other day and............,' I stumble on.

''E's had an accident', says Mrs O, leaning on the balcony rail and looking at the archway. She looks around and gives me a kind of apologetic look. ''E was knocked over there.'

'I was away last night and haven't seen him. He's in hospital,' I add.

'My God. How is he?'

'Not too good, they say,' says Mrs O.

'Have you been to see him, Unc?' asks Lily.

'Uh, no, I've only just heard about it. I've just got back.'

'Well don't let me keep you,' says Lily, jumping up. 'You'd better go.'

'Ah, well my car's in the garage having a new clutch....'

'Where's the hospital?'

'Viterbo,' supplies Mrs O.

'Isn't that on the way to Spoleto?'

'Aye,' says Mrs O. 'It is. About forty kilometres away.'

'Well, I have to be in Spoleto this evening so I can drop you off, and we can catch up on the way. Perfect. What time is it now?' She looks at her watch. 'Half past two.'

'Perrfect,' echoes Mrs O with rather a mischievous smile. They both look at me expectantly.

Viterbo, June 13th. 3pm

Everything is white. I open my eyes very slowly, because it hurts. Both the opening and the light hurts. In fact my whole head hurts, and somewhere else, but I can't tell where. I'm in a room that's very white and bright, with some kind of electronic bleeping. It's a hospital room. I'm alone, I think. I can't for the life of me think what I'm doing here, or where here is. I can sense there's a window to my left and try to turn my head to look but I can't. I try to work out why I'm here and what happened to me, but it's a bit of a blur. It's as if my brains won't focus. I remember dropping Jo off at the airport but I can't remember where she was going. I remember setting off of my bike somewhere but can't remember where. Probably somewhere on a job. I need to get my phone and talk to Jo. But I can't move much and don't know where my clothes are. Bit by bit, I become more aware of my surroundings. I don't think I'm alone after all. Behind a sort of screen on my right I think there's someone else. I can hear the breathing. I try to say something but no sound comes out. I have dreams like that sometimes, when I go to yell out because of some awful danger, but I can't get the sound out, no matter how I try. Nightmares, I suppose, rather than dreams. It's a horrible feeling. I lie here feeling helpless.

In a while a woman comes in, dressed in white. She's a nurse. She bends over and looks at me and smiles. I smile back at her, or at least I hope I do. I can't be sure because my face feels so tight. She says something. It's in a foreign language. I think it's Italian. I don't know a word of Italian. What on earth am I doing in Italy? I manage to say something now. I tell her I want to phone my wife, and I want my phone. She smiles at me again but shakes her head and says something else in Italian. I can only repeat that I want my phone. She holds up a finger. She must mean that I must wait a minute. She peeks behind the screen and leaves. It's quite a while before she comes back. There's a doctor with her, or someone who looks like a doctor. On his forehead he's wearing a band with a little lamp on the front. Like they have in cartoons to show someone's a doctor. It's the first time I've seen one. I thought they only existed in cartoons. He speaks English. Asks me how I feel. I say I can't move and ask what happened. He says I was knocked off my bike by a car yesterday, in a village a few miles away. In Graddoli. Not sure how it's spelt. He asks me what I was doing there and I say I have no idea. He says I have a broken femur, bad concussion and a small skull fracture. They are serious injuries. I have a long way to go. I'll be in hospital for quite a while. How long? They can't say exactly. Weeks rather than days. I ask if my wife knows. He turns to the nurse and speaks to her in Italian. He turns back to me and says they tried to inform her. They got my address from my driving licence and got the phone number from enquiries. They've tried a few times but it's always on answerphone. They didn't think it a good idea to leave a message. My mobile is switched off or broken. I say I must have it. Must call her. He says they'll get someone who can help me with that. I must get lots of rest. They leave. All I can hear is the bleeping. I can't hear the breathing anymore. Things start to go black.

En route for Viterbo, July 13th. 3pm

'You mean you've blamed David for all these years?' asks Lily, as she drives her swish rented Alfa Romeo wildly along the rough lane that skirts the lake from Gradoli and is a short cut to the Viterbo road. I was already feeling weird after the events of the last day or two and this violent shaking is doing nothing to help.

'Steady on,' I say.

'OK,' she says, but keeps her foot near the floor.

I was going to leave the whole matter where it was, but Lily now clearly wants to get things straight in her own head. She quickly put the whole thing behind her and has been quite successful, even if her career has stopped somewhat short of international stardom. So in fact it did her career no harm at all, proving the old adage about bad publicity.

'Yes,' I say gloomily, 'I did blame him.'

Things have turned around so quickly. Now Lily appears to be on David's side. I feel I have to explain.

'He came round that Saturday morning when you left your old flat. Remember? The filofax page where I'd just written down Nat's address went missing. The next day your picture was in the paper with his by-line on it.'

'But he can't have known Nat's address, because he didn't go there that day, and neither did I,' says Lily. 'Nat was away until the Saturday evening, and I didn't have a key. So I spent the day with that friend, who told her boyfriend where I was, and that's where the photograph was taken, when I was on my way there.'

'But when you rang that morning you said you'd moved in with Nat,' I protest, remembering the whole episode vividly.

'Well, I must have said "I'm moving in with Nat," or something like that, and you assumed I was already there.' Lily is very insistent.

'But wasn't the photo taken in Nat's street?'

'No, in my friend's street. She lived in Islington too, nearby. I suppose the streets are very similar. By the time I got there, there were already a couple of photographers. Word gets around. David was there too. I remember seeing him. He got the best shot. I saw it in the paper the next day. As you know, I felt my life was at an end. But I didn't blame him. I certainly didn't blame you. But it shows he didn't have Nat's address because he was outside my friend's flat.'

My God, she's right. Unless he turned up at Nat's and *then* got the word that she was somewhere else. But surely that's grasping at straws.

'Is that why you haven't seen David in all this time?'

I nod bleakly.

'God, that's terrible, for a friendship to end over a little thing like that. And it wasn't even true.'

'I know,' I say.

Lily is giving the whole thing its proper perspective, making me realise that there never had been any betrayal. It just existed in my head, and in my heart.

'He must have come here to clear the air with you. After all these years.'

Up till now I've been playing with the idea of going as far as the hospital with her then doubling back as soon as she left. I was still unable to face him. But this puts a different complexion on things. If only we're in time.....

'Put your foot down!' I yell.

Lily looks at me suspiciously. Jesus. What a day. What else? My phone rings. It's Mrs O. The police have been round again.

'What exactly do they want?' I ask.

'They. Want. To. Speak. To. You,' says Mrs O, enunciating slowly as if I might have trouble understanding basic English.

'Why?'

'Well, 'e had yourr name on 'im, didn't 'e?

'So?'

'So maybe they want to trrace 'is next of kin.'

175

There's the slightest of pauses.

'And they still 'aven't found out who rran 'im over yet.'

'How can I help them? I wasn't even there.'

'Well....,'

'Well, what?'

'They werre asking all kinds of questions about when you left yesterday. I didn't want to lie to them.'

'Why should you? What did you tell them?'

'I said you left the 'ouse arrownd half past ten. The man was knocked down just after quarter to eleven. They've been asking questions rrownd 'erre but no-one admits to seeing anything. They say 'e was hit by a car coming out of the square.'

'But I didn't see a thing. Jesus Christ! Surely they don't think that I............?'

'They'rre just asking questions, that's all'

'So should I go to see them after the hospital?'

'Uh, they'rre on their way to the 'ospital now.'

Bloody hell. Now I really feel hunted.

'Is it that urgent?'

'Well, they wanted your mobile number. Bu' I said I didn't 'ave it.'

'Why did you say that?'

'Because I thought that would give me time to warrn you.'

'Warn me? What do you mean, warn me? Good God. *You* think I had something to do with it, don't you?

'Look, I don't think any such thing. I don't know anything. All I'm saying is that the police are coming to the 'ospital in Viterbo. They'rre going to ask you questions. Don't do anything stupid.'

Viterbo, July 13th. 3.30pm

I come to again. I feel a bit better this time. There's a different nurse sitting at the foot of the bed. She looks at me and smiles, and then reaches towards me. She's small and pretty with lively eyes. She picks up my mobile phone from the bedside table. She puts it in front of my face. She asks me in English if I want to phone my wife, but when I try to picture Jo I can't see her face very clearly. The nurse says she'll help me if I show her what to do. I say yes.

She moves closer and puts her elbows on the bed and leans in towards me so we can both see the keypad. It's a pleasant sensation.

'Button on top,' I say. She presses it.

'Code?' she asks. I reel it off, having no problem remembering it, although other things are foggy.

'Contacts,' I say.

She nods.

'Jo,' I say.

She seems to find her way around it easily enough, pressing the scroll key rapidly. She must have a phone like it. She gives a little squeal of delight and shows me Jo's number. I give a little nod, but it hurts so much I close my eyes. I feel her hand on my arm.

'Try not to move,' says the gentle voice, 'just talk.'

I open my eyes again carefully and the room is swimming a bit, with mores floating across my vision.

'I call her?' she asks.

'Yes please.'

'What's her second name?'

'Arthur.'

'I talk first, or you?'

'You.'

She presses the key and I can hear it ringing. She glances at me with a nervous smile. I'm very nervous too. I hear a voice on the other end.

'Mrs Arser?' asks the nurse. I hear what must be a yes. 'I'm with your husband. He's OK, but he has an accident. He's in hospital in Italy.'

Slight pause. Very good, I think. Reassuring. They must get training in this. Giving information succinctly.

'He has injuries on the head and the leg,' the nurse is saying.

'In a moment you may talk to the doctor. You want to speak to your husband now?'

She holds the phone to my unbandaged year.

'Hello, David?' enquires Jo's voice, anxious but controlled.

180

'Hello Jo.' I can see her face now, and have a pang of longing.

'How are you feeling?'

'None too clever. Feeling a bit sorry for myself. But I'm OK. They're saying I'll be here for weeks.'

'What are the injuries?'

'Concussion, I think, and a broken leg.'

'Where are you?'

'I'm in........' I glance at the nurse.

'Viterbo.'

'I'm in Viterbo,' I say.

'Not far from Rome,' adds the nurse.

'Not far from Rome,' I repeat.

'I'll talk to the doctor in a minute and he can tell me how to get there. I'm back in London now. I can catch the next plane.'

'You needn't,' I say. I don't know why. I can't wait to see her.

'Of course I'm bloody coming. But what on earth were you doing there?'

'I've no idea. Lots of things are a bit hazy.'

'Well, take care. I'm looking forward to seeing you.'

'Me too. Bye.'

'Bye for now. Get some rest.' Slight pause. 'Love you.'

'Love you too.' I give an embarrassed glance at the nurse but she's taking no notice. I hand the phone back to her.

'I find the doctor and call you again,' she says into it. 'Goodbye.'

'Thank you,' I say, and relax back on my pillow. I'm exhausted but before I drift off I think to myself, 'why *am* I in Italy? Good question.'

Viterbo, July 13th. 3.45pm

It's only as Lily and I approach the hospital that my thoughts turn to the last time I was here, when K was ill. Dying in fact. Just before she came home. I'm overcome with emotion and have to stare out of the window to compose myself and not let Lily see. As I do so I see two blue *Caribinieri* cars parked near the entrance. I feel as if I'm going to pass out, as if I'll never make it.

Lily has found a parking space and is saying something - leaning forward and asking me if I'm alright. I nod, take a deep breath and try to steady my nerves. I get out slowly. It's hot still, oppressive. The trees and bushes around the hospital seem dusty and droopy, in tune with my mood.

Lily clutches my elbow to guide me in, sensing perhaps that I'm feeling unwell or that I'm dreading what lies ahead. She's right on both counts and I let her usher me, whereas in other circumstances I might have shaken her off. But it makes me feel like a condemned man being taken to meet his fate.

'Hadn't you better get going for Spoleto?' I ask her as we make our way steadily towards the reception.

'I've got plenty of time,' she says breezily. 'It's only an hour from here, isn't it?'

'About that.'

'Well, let's get you sorted out first.'

At reception we get directed to the intensive care unit, on the first floor towards the back of the hospital. It's not anywhere near where K was, thank God. We find it and go through swing doors to a small waiting room with a reception desk in the corner next to another set of swing doors. I assume these lead into the intensive care part, although as I've never been in such a unit I wouldn't really know. The nurse at the desk there does not look up when I give his name.

'Relative?'

'No.'

'Friend?'

There's just the slightest of pauses before I answer 'Yes' and I feel myself blush for some reason. I glance over at Lily but she's paying no attention.

'Has he had any other visitors?' I ask.

'I believe his wife is on her way. Take a seat.'

I follow her instructions and Lily brings us over plastic cups of water from the cooler. It's deliciously cold and I drink greedily, realising how thirsty I am. It hits the mark as only cold water can when you're so dehydrated.

We sit there for ages, chatting. At least there's no sign of any police. Lily tells me more about Lucrezia Borgia. By the time she was thirteen she'd been betrothed twice, but her ruthlessly ambitious father called them both off. After he became Pope Alexander VI he arranged her marriage with the son of a powerful Milanese family. It was the first of many: when they'd served their purpose her husbands seemed to disappear or die in mysterious circumstances. She died giving birth to her eighth child.

While I find all this interesting, I have to admit to a certain distraction and tune out at various points. Twice I ask the receptionist when I can see him and she says they'll be with me as soon as they can.

Eventually the doors swing open with a bang and two cops stride in. They make a beeline for me – we're the only people there – and ask for my name and address. Do I know this man, they ask, and show me David's driving licence. I say yes, I'm here to visit him.

He's unconscious at the moment, says the bigger cop, while the other jots in a little notebook. He was knocked down by a car yesterday morning at about quarter to eleven. Did I see him? No. Was I expecting him? No. Did I know he was in the area? No.

I'm conscious of a slight deception here, as Mrs O had told me someone was looking for me, and it had to be him. But technically I did not *know* he was in the area, I reason to myself. I only suspected.

The cop presses on. When did I last see him? About seven years ago. How long had we been friends before that? About eighteen years. Why had I not seen him in all that time? We moved to Italy, he's in London. Why did we move to Italy? For my wife's health. Where is she now? She's dead. Was there any other reason why we lost contact? No argument? Well, a slight argument. Just one of those things between friends. What about? I thought he took some damaging pictures of my niece here. He's a photographer. But I was wrong. They look at Lily, and she smiles sweetly.

Where was I at quarter to eleven yesterday morning? I was taking my car to the garage. The cop taking notes suddenly stops, and exchanges a meaningful look with his colleague. I begin to see that things are stacking up against me, that a strange picture is emerging which has nothing to do with the truth. There's a palpable tension in the room. Lily senses it too, and slips her arm through mine. The cop takes up his questioning again, this time in a quieter, almost menacing tone.

'What was wrong with your car?'

I feel as if I'm shaking slightly, and struggle to keep my voice steady.

'The clutch had gone. You can check it out. It's at the Petronelli's garage in Gradoli.'

'Oh, be assured, Sir,' he says with a sneering smile, 'we'll check it out. May I see your documents, Sir?'

I usually keep the documents in the glove compartment of the car, but recall that I took them with me when I left the car at the garage and still have them in my jacket pocket. I hand them over, feeling relieved that I can meet at least one of their demands. He reads them carefully, taking a long time. Lily clutches me more tightly.

'A blue Fiat Punto,' he says slowly, emphatically, and hands them to the note-taker who duly writes down the details. He keeps the documents.

'Where did you go after you left your car at the garage?'

'I went to Bolsena, and then I got the boat to the Isola Bisentina.'

'The Isola Bisentina?' He raises his eyebrows 'What did you do there?'

'I just needed to get away for a couple of days.'

'Isn't there some kind of monastery there?'

'It used to be. Now it's a hotel.'

'Did you tell anyone where you were going?'

'Uh, no. It was a spur of the moment thing. I didn't know where I was going myself until I got there. Then they took my mobile phone away.'

It's becoming nightmarish, this feeling of slipping into a deep, dark hole that I can do nothing about. Whatever I say seems to push me further into it.

'How did you get to Bolsena?'

'I walked.'

'You walked?' Evident incredulity now. 'Why didn't you get a bus?'

'Well, the next one wasn't due for a while and you can't rely on them. As I told you, I needed to get a way for a while?'

'What did you need to get away from?'

The killer question. The one I have been dreading and have no ready answer for.

'You know what it's like.... Things start to get on top of you..... You have to break your routine to sort a few things out in your head?'

I knew it was pointless to expect any empathy from the cop, but I couldn't help myself. I wanted to be believed.

'Why the hurry?'

'No real hurry. But once I decided, I just wanted to get going.'

'Did anyone see you?'

'Well, they must have done. Cars were passing all the time.'

'Did you keep to the main road all the time?'

'Most of the time, yes.'

'Most of the time?'

'At one point I strolled down to the lake to see if I could walk along the water's edge to Bolsena but I couldn't so I walked back to the road. But the boatmen will remember me and the people at the hotel....'

It's too late that I remember I gave a false name at the hotel. I just hope my face isn't betraying the horror I'm feeling inside. If they do check out the hotel and find I registered in a false name, even I could see how suspicious it would look.

'And the mechanics,' I add hastily, 'the mechanics at the garage will be able to tell you the times.'

'What time did you get to the garage?'

'About eleven.'

'And what time did you leave your flat?'

'A little before half past ten.'

'That's quite a long time for you to get to the garage. How do you account for that?'

I try desperately to recall the exact sequence of events.

'Well, yes, you see I did set out in the car, then the clutch was getting worse and worse, so I turned around and took it to the garage?'

'Towards Bolsena?'

'What?'

'When you set out in the car, were you heading for Bolsena, or in the other direction?'

This I really can't recall.

'No, Bolsena,' I say assertively.

'Did anyone see you leaving the apartment?'

'Yes!' It's almost a shout, as at last I say something that can be corroborated. 'My housekeeper and her nephew were there when I left'.

Mind you, that doesn't really provide any kind of alibi. Because it's becoming increasingly obvious that that's what I need.

They turn now to Lily, and I explain that I'll have to translate as she gets her Italian out of a guide book. Lily, bless her actressy socks, steps up and gives a wonderful performance: firm, clear and utterly believable.

Yes, she knows David. No, she didn't know he was in the area. No, she hasn't seen him for many years. No, she can't remember the row over the photos – it can't have been that important. At ten thirty yesterday morning she was leaving a hotel in Florence where she had been filming and was driving towards Gradoli. Yes, the hotel would have a record of her checkout time. She must have reached Gradoli about midday. No, her uncle hadn't been expecting her. She had my address but no phone number. It would be a surprise. The housekeeper answered the door and told her that her uncle wasn't there. Yes, the housekeeper speaks English.

The cops are clearly surprised by this and I have to explain that she lived in England for many years. They resume their questioning of Lily.

The housekeeper said she didn't really know when I would be back. Lily decided to find somewhere nice to stay by the lake, and the housekeeper recommended Bolsena. Yes, she found a nice hotel there. She spent the afternoon walking by the lake and looking round the town, the castle and the Basilica of Saint Catherine. In the evening she ate at the restaurant on the lake. She's now on her way to Spoleto for a few days' filming, before going on to Cinecitta in Rome. Yes, she has a hire car. Yes, it's outside now. Yes, all the documents are inside.

The questioner now turns to the note-taker and tells him to go out and inspect the car and documents with Lily and get all her details. I explain this to Lily. She squeezes my hand and they leave.

There's quite a pause. We're still standing up in the waiting room near our seats. Now the questions have stopped I can hear the normal sounds of hospital: the squeak of rubber soles on polished floors as people rush around quietly, the crash of trolleys through swing doors, the distant beeping of equipment. He addresses me quite formally and politely.

'We're doing some tests on the motorbike right now. We'll soon be able to find out if it was hit by a car, and if so, we can get a sample of the paint and determine what kind of car it was. We'll also be checking the garage to ascertain the precise nature of the repairs.'

'It's the clutch, I told you.'

'It may be the clutch, or it may be something else.'

'Like what?'

'Like a dent.' I see what he's getting at.

'Look, am I being accused of something?'

He uses the Italian equivalent of 'wanting to eliminate me from their enquiries.' While they're doing this, they'll hang on to my documents. Just a day or two. The car can stay in the garage. He advises me not to leave my address for a while. They may want to ask more questions. I ask when I will be able to see the patient. He's still unconscious, but I can stay here and wait and the hospital staff will keep me updated. His wife is arriving later tonight.

Lily returns with the other cop who nods at his colleague. I ask him if she's free to go. He says yes, but she must make herself available to them if they have any further questions. They have all her details.

He turns back to me and says that his colleague will be waiting outside the hospital to take me home whenever I want. No doubt he'll also be waiting for when David regains consciousness and get in there first to question him.

'What if I want to make my own way back?' I ask, just to test the waters.

'I wouldn't advise that, Sir. We're offering you a car. It wouldn't look good for you if you refused.'

They take their leave, thanking us for our time and co-operation. They're polite but unsmiling. I can't bring myself to say anything to them, so just nod, as does Lily.

We sit back down, speechless for a while. I'm exhausted, shattered. I look at my watch. It's now gone six o'clock. I think Lily has some kind of briefing and cast dinner in Spoleto at seven and it's about time she left. I tell her so and she starts to protest.

'There's absolutely no point in your staying here,' I say, as blithely as I can. Deep down, I would love her to stay.

'It may be ages before he comes round. I'm fine waiting, and his wife will be here soon. You've got things to do. Off you go.'

She gives my hand a little squeeze, and seems close to tears herself now. It's odd how close we so suddenly seem, whereas just a few hours ago we were relative strangers.

'And Lily, I just want to say for the record I had nothing whatsoever to do with the accident.'

'Sssh,' she says, 'you needn't say anything.'

We hug and promise to be in touch soon, and give each other little waves as she backs down the corridor.

When she's gone I sink back down in my chair, grateful to be alone for a moment but then the next moment I feel overwhelmed by the feeling of being utterly alone in the universe, for now and forever. Tears well up in my eyes, and I lean forward and bury them in my hands.

I've never felt quite like this before, but realise all of a sudden that I've been lonely for some time, not just solitary as I thought, and as I thought I wanted to be. I'd been using my solitude as a shield, against the loss of K, the rift with David, against anyone who would one day leave. And I've been unhappy, while telling myself I was not, although deep down I think I knew.

And now Jo. Jo's on her way. Who would I see first, David or Jo? What would I say? How could I apologise?'

I must have nodded off. It's gone nine now. I look around and see there's a different receptionist. I walk up to her and ask if I can see David; I've been waiting for a long time. She looks severe, with short-cropped white hair and startling red glasses, but she's friendly. It makes such a difference to find a friendly soul at times such as these. She seems to know all about him without so much as glancing at the computer.

'There's no change, I'm afraid,' she says with a smile. 'He still hasn't come round again. His wife's expected in a couple of hours.'

I manage a weak smile of thanks.

'You look done in,' she says, taking a good look at me. 'There's a cafeteria on the ground floor by the main entrance. Why don't you go and get something to eat? Give me your phone number. I'll ring you if there's any change. And if the doctor comes round I'll ask him if he can see you.'

Her kindness almost sets me off again. I give her my number and thank her warmly. She's right, I probably could do with something inside me, although I don't feel hungry. I've only had that bit of spaghetti since breakfast – *this* morning, was it? Seems an age.

I trudge down to the cafeteria: sad places in hospitals full of glum, anxious, drained faces, often with no-one to talk to. While I'm standing in the queue, I notice one woman in particular, sitting by herself in the corner. She's not that old, but looks old. Her skin is dry and pale and her eyes are red. She's pushing her pasta around on her plate with her fork and wiping her mouth all the time with her napkin, even though she's putting nothing in it. Every time someone passes she looks up, like an animal caught in a trap. I wonder who she's here for. Husband? Child? Parent? Child, I decide in the end. Her pain seems so great.

I get a large cup of black coffee, fizzy water, a toasted ciabatta sandwich and an orange, take the tray and sit at one of the tall round tables which serve only to highlight the transient, lonely nature of the place. I munch away on the food, looking around me in an effort to stop myself brooding on the current state of affairs.

Through the large windows I can see in the fading light a cop car parked just outside the main door, where I was before. There's someone in it, but I can't tell if it's the note-taker. I consider going out to tell him I'm going to be a while longer. I could also ask him if there's any news on the tests on the bike, or if they've spoken to the garage about my car. But I think better of it. No news is good news and all that. Best left alone.

I have my phone on the table, waiting for the receptionist's call, for news of David. It's silent. I suddenly think I should call Mrs O to let her know what's going on and I do.

'Arre you in some kind of trrwble?' she asks, when I tell her about the police.

I tell her not to worry, it's only that they're trying to find out what happened, David's still unconscious, and I don't have an alibi. I admit to her that it's looking a bit suspicious because I'm the only one here who knows him, apart from Lily, who was leaving the Florence hotel at the time of the accident. Why isn't anyone coming forward with information, I ask.

'Now, don't go getting yourself in a mooddle,' says Mrs O. 'You know how they drrive rrownd 'erre. Bloody maniacs. 'E probably just swerved to avoid someone and hit the kerb or swmmat.'

'He's a very good driver. And the police seem to think he was hit by a car. Have you seen any of them around asking questions this afternoon?'

Mrs O says she hasn't. I'm not sure whether that's good or bad. But the whole thing sounds much more simple and straightforward when she says it. Just one of those everyday things, not the dark mystery the police seem to think it is.

Mrs O offers to come round tomorrow, not one of her regular days, and cook us a nice lunch. I jump at the chance.

'It'll all seem so much better in the morning,' she says.

Mrs O. What would I do without her. With the food and her wise words of comfort I do feel considerably better already.

'His wife will be arriving before long,' I say, thinking more clearly now. 'She'll need somewhere to stay. I'll ask her back.'

'That's a good idea. The spare rroom's all made up nice. I did it when I thought yourr niece might want to stay.'

I walk back along the corridor to the lift with renewed resolve in my step, the readier to face whatever has to be faced. When I get back to the waiting area at intensive care, Jo is there talking to the nice nurse with the white hair and red glasses.

Jo looks elegant, immaculate and worried. She's hardly changed at all in the years since I've seen her, except that her short hair is sprinkled with grey and white at the temple like a first smattering of snow. It looks so distinguished against her gleaming black skin. Why is it that grey never looks this good on white people?

She notices me, we sort of freeze for an instant, and as we walk towards each other there's an odd, slow motion feel about it like a bad film. Yet it happens in a flash. In the cafeteria I'd been rehearsing what I'd say to her when she came, but of course I don't manage to get any of it out.

'How *good* it is to see you,' she says, taking both my hands in hers, and I can tell she means it. I think how gracious she is in the circumstances. 'It's been a long, long time.'

'How is he?' is all I can say.

'Still unconscious. I've been sitting with him for a while.' She looks at me, trying to say something.

'He's not out of the woods yet. He's just lying there like a lifeless thing. Like a statue. '

We hug. I can feel her shaking slightly in my arms. I remember how fond of her I always was.

'I'm sorry. I'm sorry,' I say over and over.

Jo composes herself and we separate, a little awkward now. She asks me what I'm sorry for.

'For everything. It's all my fault.'

'What do you mean? What do you think is your fault?' she asks gently.

'Everything. The fact that he came here, the accident, that stupid quarrel in the first place. I was in the wrong. I know that now.'

'Now, now. You mustn't blame yourself.'

I sense that the last thing she needs is me feeling sorry for myself, and try to pull myself together. I want to tell her about the police and their suspicions, make a clean breast of it as it were. I ask her down for some coffee but she doesn't want to leave. The doctor's told her the next couple of hours could be crucial. She suggests I go and get some coffee and bring it into her in David's room, so I can see him for a while. She says she knows he'd want that.

I check with the nurse, and she says it will be alright for a moment or two. When I come back with the coffees, the policeman who was taking the notes is standing by the reception desk. He nods at me. The nurse opens the double doors and nods towards one of the four doors that lead from a little corridor. I've never been in intensive care, not even when K was ill, and I don't know quite what to expect. Maybe I have a vague image of oxygen tents, tubes and monitors.

It's not quite like that – just a small room with two beds. One is empty. Jo is sitting beside the other, holding David's hand which lies motionless at his side. His face is half-hidden with bandages, but I'd still have recognised him. It feels unreal somehow. Another nurse is sitting in the corner. She quickly and quietly pulls up another chair for me near Jo.

I give Jo one of the coffees and proffer the other to the nurse. She smiles, shakes her head and returns to her chair. I sit down next to Jo. The visible part of David's face looks peaceful, almost happy.

'Do you think he can hear us?' I whisper to Jo, wondering if there's any need to. But it seems the thing to do.

'You never know, do you? They say you should act as if they could. I've been talking to him, telling him what I've been doing, and the fact that you're here.'

She smiles down at him, but it's not a tearful, simpering smile. It's a strong smile, with almost a twinkle in it, as if to say, 'Come on you old bugger. On your feet, and we'll go and knock back a few for old times' sake'. I'm transported back to the old times for a moment, when friendship and companionship and trips to the pub were taken for granted. Jo turns to me.

'He came round for a little while earlier,' she says. 'I did manage to speak to him briefly. He couldn't remember what he was doing here. In fact the doctor says there may to be gaps in his memory for quite a while'.

'So he doesn't remember anything about the accident?'

'No, nothing at all.'

So he won't be able to exonerate me, at least for the time being. But it could also mean...... Jo interrupts my thoughts, and voices them.

'Maybe it's time finally to let bygones be bygones and get on with life.'

'Yes. You're right.'

'I'm sure you'd appreciate some time alone with him. Just to say hello properly.'

I go to protest but she says she needs to go to the bathroom anyway, and is up out of her chair. I move up into her seat, feeling foolish. I can't quite bring myself to hold his hand, so I rest mine on his forearm. At first I stumble over a few commonplace phrases about being pleased to see him. Soon though, it all comes tumbling out: how I'd just found out that he couldn't have taken that missing page, that maybe there was never a missing page because I hadn't written the address down in the first place - just thought I had – that I was wrong not to trust him, that for years I'd harboured an anger that I thought was for him, had wallowed in self-pity and nursed myself with pride, but what I was really doing was grieving. By the time I finish I notice my hand is gripping his, and a couple of tears have sploshed down on them.

As I dry my eyes and sit back, the door opens and in comes Jo. Maybe she's been waiting there until I was done. When she sits down, I say, 'There are things I need to tell you.'

'No there aren't,' she says softly. 'At least not now.'

She's right. It's late, almost midnight, and this is not about me. I offer her a bed but she says she'll stay here. The nurse has said she can use the spare bed. We swap numbers and she assures me that she'll ring me if there's any change. We hug again tightly, all awkwardness gone. When I go into the waiting area, the cop has gone. He's probably had a quick word with Jo. So I walk to the main entrance to see if he's waiting for me. He is.

Gradoli, July 14th. 6.30am

The rising sun is spreading its pinky glow over the town, and a water mist blankets the valley and the lake below. It looks like a glossy picture from a tourist brochure, the kind of scene you don't see in real life. There's a kind of promise in the air, but also some dark clouds coming in from the sea, threatening to spoil the day.

I'm standing at the kitchen window surveying all this, pepping myself up with strong coffee and a cigarette after a restless night. I kept waiting for the phone to ring, but it could have been good news or bad news, so I didn't know whether I wanted it to ring or not. The silence means there is no news, which is probably better. Yet I do want it to ring. I want to hear that David will be OK.

Now it's daylight I feel worse: isolated, useless, daunted by the long day ahead. I have to stop myself ringing Jo because she might be grabbing a couple of hours' sleep. I mooch around the house trying to find something to do. Then I remember I can now have a hot bath for the first time in ages, because Rossano came and fixed it a century or so ago, it seems. In fact, when I come to think about it, I can't be sure it really has been fixed. So much has happened since then. Wasn't there some part or other he needed?

When I do go and try the bath it's a great joy when the hot water comes gushing out. How we appreciate things when they've been gone for a while. I try to relax in the steaming bath with classical music on the radio. It doesn't work very well. My mind keeps going over all that happened in the last couple of days, and what might happen.

My car! It should be ready today. When the cop brought me back last night he told me they'd finished with it and I could pick it up when I wanted to. That's good news, isn't it? Something to be pleased about. It means they haven't found any dents, doesn't it? That they can rule me out of their investigations. Doesn't it? The truth is, I don't really know. Don't know what they've found. I can't start celebrating just yet.

The cop had advised me again not to stray too far away. What about the hospital in Viterbo, I asked. That would be OK, he said.

I think the garage opens at eight o'clock. So after more caffeine and nicotine I stroll up there. The metal shutter, which K would have called the portcullis, is still down but there are sounds coming from within so I bang on the window. A mechanic emerges from the small metal door in the big metal door, wiping his hands on a dirty rag. He looks sullen, and I have to describe my car and what was wrong with it and when I brought it in. He tells me to wait a minute.

He goes inside, then comes back out of the same door and walks up the street. I wonder if he's forgotten about me. I lean against the garage wall smoking, this latest desertion just adding to my sense of remoteness, of disassociation.

This is my fourth cigarette this morning, and it's not even nine o'clock. I've cut down quite a bit in the last few months, and recently have been down to two a day. One with my evening drink on the balcony, and one after dinner. All that's gone out of the window now. In fact I'm almost out. I need some more.

I see my car coming down the street. The mechanic pulls up in front of the garage and gets out.

'The cops came looking for this yesterday,' he says.

'I know.'

'Did some tests'

'Oh, yes? Did they find anything?'

'Don't know. Any trouble?'

'Something about an accident in the town a couple of days ago. They wanted to rule me out.'

'*Ah, si*. They brought the bike here too. It's in a right mess. It's a very old one. English.'

'Did they ask any questions?'

'Might have asked the boss a couple.'

'Can I see the bike?' I ask on impulse. Of course it would be an old bike if David were driving it. Oddly, it's this image more than anything that brings memories flooding back, and I feel quite emotional. I think of the friendship I've missed out on for all these years, and the world I shut out as a consequence. It's all I can do to continue the conversation.

'Better not,' says the mechanic. 'They wouldn't like it.'

No doubt the whole story has gone round Gradoli by now, which makes it all the more curious that no-one has come forward to say anything. Maybe it was someone who was driving without insurance or something like that – someone who wanted nothing to do with the police.

I settle the bill. For once it's actually less than the sum they'd originally quoted. I drive home feeling slightly buoyed by this. I proceed towards the arch much more carefully than usual. It's at the end of a cobbled side street, set back a little way. The other side of the arch the road swings sharply up to the left, as the level of the *piazza* is higher than the street level, and sharply down to the right and the parking bay beneath the wall. So it is a bit of a blind spot, and there's room for only one file of traffic under the arch itself. I've had near misses myself before now. But everyone seems to stop in time before hitting anything.

There's nothing coming through the arch. A couple of crones with shopping bags are walking across the grass of the *piazza* towards it. I park the car in the usual place below the front wall and find myself walking over to the arch for a look. The accident happened just inside the arch, I remember the cops saying. Or was it Mrs O? I don't know what I expect to find. The police must have been over it with a fine toothcomb. They can't have missed anything.

There is something there though. Something the police could not take with them. A skid mark. A single skid mark. It must be have been made by a motorbike. It starts just inside the arch, then swerves sharply towards the left and peters out before the wall. That means he was hit by a car coming up from the parking bay, or swerved to avoid it, or someone. But it's more likely to be a car coming up from the parking bay, as anyone walking up from it would be likely to be going across the *piazza,* to one of the flats. In any case they would have heard the motorbike coming and kept out of harm's way. The police must have worked all this out. That's why they think he was hit by a car.

I'm unnerved by this and come over a bit wobbly again. Another couple of crones pass me on the grass and although they sing *Buongiorno* I can't help feeling they're looking at me rather suspiciously.

When I open the door to the flat there's a strong smell of coffee, toast and cigarettes. Mrs O is leaning over the sill of the kitchen window as I had done a couple of hours ago. Rarely have I been so glad to see anyone in all my life.

'Is it your day?' I ask.

'I told you yesterday I'd come over. You're prrobably not feeding yourself prroperly, are you? I've made you a bit o' brreakfast.'

I sit down at the kitchen table and tuck into the toast and boiled eggs. Mrs O sits opposite me drinking coffee – she hardly ever seems to eat anything despite her constant efforts to force-feed everyone else – and watches me in a satisfied way.

'Mrs O, there's something you ought to know.'

'No, therre isn't,' she says, shaking her head.

I'm relieved but infuriated at the same time. How is it that when after all this time I finally want to talk to people, nobody wants to listen? Maybe it's because they don't want to hear me confess anything, but I want to tell them I had nothing to do with the accident.

'Me sisterr's going downhill fast,' she says, bringing me back down to earth with a bump. It's not all about me, I say to myself again. 'She's not long for this world.'

'I'm so sorry to hear that,' I say. She shrugs.

'Should you be here?'

'She's asleep, and a neighbourr's sitting in wi' 'er. It'll be a few days yet. Any rroad, I have to get out of the 'ouse now and again.'

I tell her that David is still in a coma and I'm waiting for a phone call from Jo.

'Well, I think you should get over therre anyway,' she says. 'I'll hold the fort 'erre, never fear.'

My phone rings. It's on the table by my right arm. We both jump and look at it as if it's a bomb about to go off. Mrs O is the first one to come to her senses and orders me rather belligerently to answer it. It's Jo.

'Hello?' I say in a somewhat croaky voice.

'Hello there.'

Thank God, she sounds normal and cheerful.

'He's come round. He's going to be OK. Can you get over here? He's asking for you'.

I jump up and tell Mrs O he's going to be OK. I run down the stairs, feeling suddenly years younger. I don't know what makes me do it, but when I get to the car, I look around it for any bumps or scratches. It's as clean as a whistle. Despite myself I feel relieved. I set off, trying to drive sensibly but know that I'm being a little wild. I start thinking how much David will remember, and what he will have to say to me.

Viterbo, July 14th. 9am

I wake up and Jo smiles at me. I can't remember where I am but I know it's a strange place. It seems odd that Jo is here. I do remember something about an accident. I look down and see the plaster and bandages. I'm in hospital. I look at Jo and manage a weak smile. She holds my hand.

'How are you feeling?' she asks.

'Better than I was, I think. How am I doing?'

'The doctor says you've come through the worst. But it was sort of touch and go there for a while.'

'What are you doing here?'

'What a question. I came to see you of course. I was back in London and when I heard I jumped on the next plane. Do you know where we are? What you're doing here?'

'We're in Italy. I came to see Griff.'

Jo tells me that's right. She's seen him. She says he's fine, just like he used to be. He wants to come and see me, she says. I say that'll be great. She asks if I remember why I hadn't seen him for such a long time. I don't really. There was some kind of row a while ago, but the details are very hazy, like a half-remembered dream. It doesn't seem to matter now. If it ever did. It feels very good to be alive, and have Jo here. And Griff will be here soon. But why didn't I see him?

'Do you remember what happened?' Jo is asking.

'There was an accident.' It plays back now like a grainy film. 'I was trying to find Griff, but I fell off my bike. Something ran in front of me. A little dog I think. I swerved to avoid it and hit a kerb or something. Went flying. These old bikes aren't the safest of things.'

Jo is looking a bit haggard, despite her smiles. I suppose she must have been worried about me. She probably hasn't slept. She got here late last night, she says, and Griff was here. She slept in the other bed in the room. Well, she didn't sleep much. Just dozed fitfully. Griff has said she can stay at his place any time I want while I recuperate. That's good of him.

'Where's he now?' I ask.

'He went back last night. He lives about an hour away. I'll give him a call in a minute. But first the doctor will need to come in. He wanted to see you when you came round.'

Jo and I run out of things to say for a moment or two, as you do in hospital. I begin to see that it's going to be an awful long time in here. Jo will have to go back to London at some point for work.

Griff will only come in now and again. I won't be able to chat with other patients. Won't be able to read papers or listen to the radio or watch TV. Well, won't be able to understand them anyway. But I must not feel sorry for myself. I must remember that I'm lucky to be alive. I must take each day as it comes. I'm feeling better already – just a little helpless.

The doctor comes in. I think I saw him yesterday. He speaks quite good English. Jo excuses herself, saying she'll go and call Griff. The doctor is quite a nice guy, but does a lot of probing, both physically and mentally. He asks me quite a few of the same questions as Jo, about the accident and what I remember of it. I go over it again, but can't tell him any more. He ends up saying I'm doing pretty well, will mend in time, but I'm not going anywhere for a few weeks. He says the memory gaps might close a bit but not entirely. I thought as much. But he's quite reassuring. He seems to understand. He knows I have a friend living nearby. They sell English papers in Bolsena – that name sounds familiar – and my friend can bring them over. They can probably find a laptop for me to use as I get better.

'Don't worry. We'll have you on your feet again sooner than you think. And now, the police will want to ask you some questions.'

'The police?'

'Because of the accident. I'll tell them what you told me, but they will want to ask you themselves. I'll make sure they won't stay with you for too long.'

I'm beginning to tire of all these questions, but want to get it over with. When the doctor leaves Jo comes in with two cops – a man and a woman. It's the woman who does all the talking, and I go over it again. She asks if I'm sure it was a dog that ran out. Of course I'm not sure, but I think it was something little. Could I have been hit by a car? No, definitely not. Did Griff know I was coming? No.

I can see what they're getting at. They think Griff might have knocked me over. Ridiculous. I get angry and tell them so. Jo tells me to calm down. The policewoman smiles and thanks me. That will be all, and they shouldn't have to bother me again.

I'm knackered now. I'm on a drip but Jo says I can have some orange juice and has brought some. I just about manage it – it's a bit painful to get it down.

I say to Jo I could do with a nap and she says good, she'll go for some lunch in the cafeteria. Griff is on his way over and they'll come in when I wake up.

I do so a couple of hours later, feeling better. I'm alone, and for a while at least it's quite welcome after this morning's shenanigans. I take time to reflect on it all. There's nothing much to add. I do now remember being in a tent by a lake, thinking I would go and see Griff but not being sure what reception I would get. I was worried about it. So there must have been some bad blood between us. I don't know what it was all about anymore. I don't care. I do know that I have been lucky. I'm alive, and will in time have use of brain and body.

Jo puts her head round the door.

'How's the patient?' she asks.

She's looking a bit better now herself. Perhaps she had a nap too. I tell her I'm feeling better.

'Up to seeing a visitor?'

'Bring him in,' I say.

She does. It's bloody good to see him. He hasn't changed all that much. A little greyer, a little heavier, but the same old Griff. In contrast to Jo he looks uptight and sort of......emotional. He goes to shake my hand, but then realises that I can't raise it from the bed, so he does this little awkward movement where he reaches down and lifts up my fingers in a one-handed shake. He looks embarrassed but it makes me chuckle, and then he chuckles too so it sort of breaks the ice. I can't wait for the old, witty, sarcastic Griff to come back.

He's still a bit awkward though and doesn't seem to know what to say. I suppose men visiting mates in hospital usually don't. And it's been a long time.

'So how've you been doing?' he says eventually.

'Have been better,' I say, 'but I'll live.'

'Well, you will get better. It'll just take a bit of time. But I'm not far away.'

'I'll do my best.'

'You'd better. Hurry up out of here, so we can have that pint. Your round, I believe.'

And then we're off, chatting away like in the old days, as if nothing had happened, and we didn't have a care in the world.

Positano, October

When I got back later that afternoon, after seeing David, the flat was empty. I was expecting Mrs O to be there, but she wasn't. Alarm bells rang. So I called her on the mobile. Her sister died just after lunchtime. Mrs O said she'd been expecting her to fight on a bit longer, but she was very weak from all the pain. I offered my condolences, and she said she was in a better place, although I know she's not a believer. I asked her if she wanted me to go round, but she said Francesca's son and daughter were there and were taking care of everything.

Mrs O sounded composed and resigned. She asked how my friend was doing.

'Not too bad,' I said. 'He's out of the coma and the doctor said he should be fine but it'll take time. He's got a positive attitude, and that's half the battle.'

'Aye,' said Mrs O, 'that's half the battle. So is everrything alrright between you now?'

'Yes, everything's alright.'

'Good. And now I'm going to pour meself a stiff whisky.'

Like her sister, Francesca had been a small, strong feisty woman. She'd worked herself up as a Communist trade union rep and eventually became housing director for the district. She was always scrupulously fair, working within the rules to the letter, but whenever she could she'd make sure the neediest of people got the benefits that were their due, which is not easy in any system.

The whole of the town turned out to the funeral. Many had something to thank her for. It was a simple, moving service. I accompanied Mrs O down the aisle to the strains of the Communist anthem *La Bandiera Rossa*, as Francesca had stipulated.

When it was over I waited for her in the car. It took her a long time to greet and thank everyone. I could see her on the church steps. It was as if the town was finally accepting her, welcoming her back into the fold.

When she got in beside me, I remarked on what a beautiful service it was.

'Ahh,' said Mrs O, 'I'd have rrather gone to the picturres.'

To this day I don't know whether she meant she'd have rather gone to the pictures than have her sister die, or she'd simply have preferred to have gone to the pictures than go to the funeral. I wouldn't put it past her.

But it's funny, isn't it? How it hits you. At that moment I knew, as we followed the hearse to the cemetery on the outskirts of the town where K is buried. And three months later Mrs O and I were walking down the aisle again, arm in arm at our wedding. My own Sophia Loren.

I'd gradually regained my equilibrium. Someone once told me what Darwin meant by the survival of the fittest is in fact that the species who survive are those who can best adapt to change, not literally the fittest. I don't know whether that's true or not, but I could see now that I'd been a bit of a fossil myself for a long time in my self-imposed exile in Italy.

And when I thought about it, as I did on the way back from the hospital in Viterbo that day, I came to the conclusion that we can go badly wrong when we try to preserve the past or seek to set it in stone like Michelangelo's David, never changing or ending. When we find something we love, it's only natural to want to preserve it for all eternity. But when it doesn't work out like that, and it never can of course, we can lose our way.

The point is that it's the life in someone that we love, and life is change, and we must accept that. So we must celebrate love wherever we may find it, but not hang on to it so tightly that we squeeze the life out of it. Here endeth the final lesson.

I'm not sure, but I think Mrs O may have manoeuvred me into marriage. I wouldn't put it past her.

'Well, that's the last of them gone now,' she had said as the car crawled up the hill behind the hearse.

I knew she had a brother in Turin who she didn't like and never saw, and another sister in Bradford. Maybe she meant the last of her siblings round here. She's never one to miss the chance of a bit of melodrama.

I glanced over at her. She was looking out of the window as if we were out on a Sunday drive in the country. She was muttering, almost to herself. She was wondering what to do now. She couldn't go back to England because she'd sold the council house she'd bought under Mrs Thatcher. Francesca's flat was rented and she wasn't sure she could keep on there, or whether she wanted to.

She asked about my plans. Was I going to keep in touch with David? David was making a good recovery. Jo had been staying at my place but would have to go back to London for a while for work. She'd come back before he was discharged. I'd keep on going to Viterbo until then, of course. I'd been taking Jo over every day since the accident and fetching her in the evening. I'd see David quite often, but not for very long. Men aren't very good in hospitals at the best of times. And it was harder for us. I thought it better to proceed cautiously at first, although he didn't seem to feel any awkwardness. It was as if he just picked up where we'd left off. But I on the other hand would sometimes ponder what would happen if he suddenly remembered the whole story and could see what a complete idiot I'd been. I wouldn't blame him if he never wanted to see me again. At other times though I had a sneaking suspicion that he could remember a bit more than he was letting on.

Either way, he and Jo would leave before long. Jo had been a brick, very supportive and grateful, although I have no idea what for. She and Mrs O had got on like a house on fire.

'Your friend is so *simpatica*', she said in one of her rare reversions to her Italian with me.

Lily had rung a day or two before the funeral saying she'd call in to see me on her way back to London and *Three Sisters* at the National.

So people had come back into my life only to go away again. Suddenly the prospect of returning to my old solitary life seemed appalling, unthinkable. Mrs O and I had always got on but over the past few days we'd grown even closer.

I realised that a funeral was not the ideal place for a proposal, especially when it's your sister's. But was it totally unacceptable? Would Mrs O mind? Not if she'd prefer to be at the pictures anyway. And surely she wouldn't want a bended knee and roses? No, she was so down to earth. She'd laugh at anything overblown. But still – at a funeral?

As we stood at the graveside though, I felt I must speak now or forever hold my peace, as it were. This surge of hope and love may go away again, and I'd be trapped in my old, bad ways.

Of course I'd waited until Francesca was lowered neatly on top of her husband. Mrs O's eyes filled up, I could see, but she fought to stem the tears. That was her way.

It was still only about eleven in the morning, but already beginning to get too hot for comfort. It was a relief to get back to the air conditioning in the car. Normally I don't like air conditioning, but there are times when it's unbearable without it.

So I started the car, and when we'd cooled down a little, headed down the hill to the main road. There, it was left for Francesca's flat and right for mine. It was now or never.

'Why don't we pool our resources?' I asked her.

I could tell she knew immediately what I meant. But she said, 'I wonder if you mean what I think you mean?'

'Get hitched, get spliced, get........,' I said

'Knotted?' she said. At this we both chuckled.

'Aye, let's get knotted.'

A second or two later she said, 'Serriously though, I'd be very honoured,' and put her hand over mine.

And then, because despite her hard exterior I knew there was a romantic spot there somewhere, I turned the car around and drove to the restaurant on the lake, where we had some champagne and our first kiss. I just hope we weren't spotted by anyone who knew her sister.

I thought it would take me a while to adjust to remarried life, but from the start it just seemed right, our byroad love.

She came with me to the hospital to meet David and we broke the news. He seemed genuinely pleased. Now the bandages were off his face he was his old recognisable self. A little older of course and paler than his usual rugged, outdoorsy looks. He was charm itself to Mrs O, teasing her in a rather impish way to which she responded with schoolgirl giggles. I was delighted they hit it off.

After five weeks David was discharged and Jo came to fetch him. They spent a couple of days with us before we drove them down to

Fiumicino. We'd got the bike fixed and asked Rossano to keep it in his garage until David could come back and get it.

At the airport we all exchanged warm and even tearful hugs. They promised to come back for the wedding. And they did, along with Mrs O's sister from England and one of her daughters, and my son Jake, whom I hadn't seen since the day of K's funeral. I thought I had to tell him about Mrs O and me, and ask him to the wedding, otherwise there'd be more recriminations. I didn't think he'd come, or even approve. He didn't mention the row we'd had that day, but he was conciliatory, and stayed with us in the flat. So it was quite a convivial throng. My daughter Alex couldn't make it over from Australia, but she was glad to be asked.

We followed the service by lunch in the restaurant on the lake. Mrs O looked radiant. I suppose I should stop calling her Mrs O now. I can't adapt it to my surname as Mrs T would be out of the question. In fact I usually do call her by her first name – a beautiful name – but sometimes Mrs O slips out. When it does, we make a joke of it. We laugh quite a lot now. We can't take ourselves too seriously in our position, which is a good thing.

We drove down here to Positano for our honeymoon – another joke. Honeymooners at our age! Travelling doesn't worry me at all any more, with Mrs O by my side. David and Jo have invited us over for Christmas in Clapham, which we're both looking forward to. Mrs O has already made a plum pudding. We might even go over to Australia to see Alex and her family next year.

And in Italy we have plans to go to lots of places neither of us have ever seen. On the way here we stopped at Pompeii which we found riveting and spent all day there. We didn't want to leave. Unlike, of course, the poor buggers who were trapped there. Talk about preserving life in stone! The bodies of some of the would-be fugitives looked almost animalistic as they tried to escape the tide of lava and ash, their mouths drawn back in snarls of agony. In a way, of course, they have been immortalised, but at the worst moments of their lives, in the throes of terrible death, a moment they could never have foreseen. It made me even more grateful for the turns my own life had recently taken. Before that, I too may as well have been buried alive.

I thought back to the statue of David, and how it seems to have a vitality which these creatures lack. I mentioned it to Mrs O, and she'd had the same thought. In contrast, the town of Pompeii itself was amazingly alive: the houses, bars, theatres and brothels. You could almost hear the bustle.

As we drove around the bay to Positano, I thought about preserving what's good in life and how difficult it is to get right, just as it is in art. Michelangelo had achieved what Vesuvius couldn't. And now, somehow, I thought I had managed it too after all, just when I'd sort of given up. You can't make a rock out of your relationships, but time can make a bedrock for them to rest on.

I try not to think about the wasted years, and the mess I made of things. Sometimes you have to go through things to get to the other side. Mrs O had been with me through illness and loss and she's still by my side, solid as a rock.

We're staying high on the cliffs at Positano, in a little bed and breakfast called *La Villa Rondinaia,* which translates as The Swallows' Nest. There's a stunning view over the rocky coast, which we admire under the setting sun and the crimson sea with our drinks on the little balcony. This evening I started singing, '*When the swallows come back to Positano…*'

'It's not Positano, you fool,' says Mrs O. 'In the song.'

'What is it then?'

'Capistrrano. *When the swallows come back to Capistrrano..*'

'Capistrano? Where's Capistrano?'

'A little island. Off California.'

'I always thought it was Positano.'

'Joost shows how wrrong you can be.'

We laugh.

And so we make plans for the future, knowing that some of them may never be realised, but that some of them will. At least I use the word future now. Until recently I'd stopped saying it.

At last I've buried the past, after all those wasted years, and all over a missing scrap of paper. To this day I can't fathom what happened to it. But it doesn't matter now. The dog could have eaten it, for all I know. Some things have to remain a mystery. They never did trace the car in David's hit-and-run either. And I came that close to losing everything.

The swallows are beginning to leave, and I think of my father back on the farm in Wales telling me about the swallows who came to the barn on virtually the same day every year, and left with equal punctuality. How many have to leave, before you can say it's winter? What did Aristotle have to say about that, I'd like to know?

It doesn't matter, because they'll be back next spring. And these times will become the old times.

Printed in Great Britain
by Amazon